The Wor Child

Emily Catford
Copyright © 2021 Emily Catford

All rights reserved.

CHAPTER ONE

Annie laid back on the bed she shared with another girl and gave out a deep sigh. Her stomach grumbled as she tried not to think about how hungry and tired she was.

She'd been at the workhouse for the past six months and still couldn't believe that her father had abandoned her there. Each day she expected him to turn up, saying it had all been a mistake, but he hadn't been to visit once.

One morning he'd picked up a pillowcase, thrust her few meagre belongings inside and walked swiftly to the workhouse, dragging her behind him. She'd glanced around her as they marched down the streets, not recognising where they were going. She'd watched as her dad had kept his palm pressed down on the bell until someone had come out to see them.

He'd thrust her forward and turned quickly as though he couldn't; bare to look at her. She'd tried to pull away from the woman who held her arm tightly but matron had been too strong. She looked over her shoulder as her father walked away without a word, not even bothering to look over his shoulder one last time.

Big fat tears rolled down her cheeks as she thought back to when her mother had been alive. They hadn't had much, just a small room where the three of them lived together. There had been damp on the walls and the wallpaper had been peeling off but her mother had kept it as clean as she could, though the soot belching out of the nearby factory chimneys made sure it didn't stay clean for long.

She tried to remember her father being kind to her, but as much as she screwed up her closed eyes, her only memories of him were his gruff voice. When he entered the room, the room seemed to shrink, as did her mother.

Thinking back to before her mother died she did her best to hold back the tears. She knew she wouldn't get any sympathy if she was heard. She tried to remember

remember the good times, when she was sat with her mother, with her long blonde hair flowing over her shoulders. Her soft blue eyes crinkling at the edges as she patiently showed her daughter how to use the twine to create small posies.

She could still hear the soft murmur of her mother as she patiently sat creating the bunches of flowers that they would take to the market and sell to those that could afford the pittance she'd charged.

She'd always been so cheerful thought Annie with a bitter sweet smile as she looked around at the large room which was lined with beds against the two opposite walls, with over fifty girls sleeping, two to a bed. *I should try to be more like my mother, but it's so difficult to think of a reason to be happy when I'm living here,* she thought as she pulled her scratchy grey blanket over her scrawny shoulders.

It had been a particularly bad day. Matron had been upset because Annie had dropped the bucket she was carrying and the dirty water had slopped everywhere.

"You're a clumsy good for nothing. Clean this up now." She'd shouted.

Annie had looked up with her and held her breath, but couldn't help answering back.

"It was an accident Mrs Price." She'd said politely.

"You insolent child. Come here now." Matron told her.

For a moment Annie had been frozen to the spot. Then she forced herself to put one foot slowly in front of the other. Her whole body was trying to delay the moment she'd be within arms reach of the matron.

"I'm sorry." She stammered. "I'll clean it up now."

"You will. Now go." Matron had said, her eyes being drawn to a fight going on further down the corridor.

As Annie mopped up the spilt water, she thanked her lucky stars that some other misdeed had taken away Matron's attention, otherwise she'd probably been on the receiving end of the birch, Mrs Price's favourite punishment.

Being only seven and small for her age, Annie was often subject to bullying by some of the older children. They would tug at her dark auburn ringlets and make fun of the large dimples she had on her slightly round cheeks. Her long eyelashes that framed her big brown eyes would glisten with the tears as she tried hard to suppress would finally start flowing. Her whole body would tense and her dainty hands would clench automatically, ready to do battle with the bigger child.

Most of the time her temper cooled quickly enough for her to realise that she would come off worse if she reacted to their taunts. Occasionally, though, she'd see the red mist and she'd run at them arms flailing as she rained small punches over them, until they held her at arms length, laughing at her before sending her off with a bruise to remind her she couldn't win against these older bigger children..

At least when Sarah's there I don't have to worry, she thought as she lay there deep in thought. *She'll send them packing if she catches them at it.* She smiled as she remembered the first time that Sarah had stuck up for her.

As much as Annie had tried to slouch and hide from view they'd often corner her on the way to lessons. Catching her in the cold dark corridors, the paint peeling and the tiles cracking, they'd circle her and start to call her names and pushing her around.

"Oy." A girls voice had shouted out.

The group had stopped in surprise, all turning to where the voice had originated.

"Why don't you pick on someone your own size." The

girl had continued as she came closer.

Annie couldn't believe her luck. The girl had looked at least twelve and was obviously not scared of these bullies. The group had looked at the girl and then at each other, not knowing how to react. They weren't used to anyone standing up to them and looked to the ring leader for guidance.

His ears turned a bright red and he cleared his throat in embarrassment. He shrugged his shoulders and turned away, the rest of them following. As they reached the end of the corridor the ringleader had looked sheepishly over his shoulder before vanishing out of sight.

"You okay?" The girl had asked, with a soft smile.

Annie had nodded at her gratefully. She looked up at her saviour. Her dark brown hair was pulled into a tidy knot at her long neck. Annie couldn't help but mirror the wide grin of the girl in front of her.

"Yes, thank you. You saved my life." She remembered saying, now laughing quietly at how dramatic she'd sounded.

The girl had laughed at the exaggeration and put her hand out to shake Annies.

"I'm Sarah. I don't think I've seen you around before."

"I'm Annie. I've been here a couple of months, but I try to hide so they don't push me around." She'd explained.

"What those lot... they're just jealous, cos you are pretty." Sarah had kindly told her.

Annie looked up at her with a tentative smile. She'd never been called pretty before. She didn't realise that as she was getting older her childlike features were starting to blossom and she would soon be quite a beauty.

"Off to lessons then, I suppose." Sarah continued, and linked arms with her new friend and walked with her until they got to the classroom. Annie went to take her usual place at the back, but Sarah pulled her and together they sat near to the window.

Sarah wasn't much of a scholar and liked to look out the window and dream that someone would eventually come and take her away.

Though it was frowned upon to get too close to the other inhabitants, from that day forwards Annie and Sarah had become close friends.

With Sarah beside her, Anne felt safe and secure, but knew that being thwarted could mean that the bullying would be two-fold next time they managed to catch her unawares.

CHAPTER TWO

Fred and Martha were sat in the park, enjoying the sunshine, with a picnic. The sun was shining and the soft scent of freshly mowed lawn floated on the summer breeze.

They enjoyed the morning strolling through the meandering paths, watching the squirrels scamper across the grass and running up the trees. It was so nice that they had this a short walk from their house.

Not many people have it so lucky, Martha thought as she leaned over to pull another grape from the bunch that was sat in the middle of the blanket they had laid down on the ground to have their picnic. Martha suddenly put her hand to her stomach as she felt a strong pain rip through her lower half. She gasped and looked down to see blood seeping through her petticoats.

"Oh Fred." Martha cried. "It's happened again." She started to sob gently, the lovely day already a distant memory.

Fred looked over at her with wide eyes and followed her gaze. His mouth opened to say something but nothing came out, as he realised what she was saying.

He shook his head as he realised that his first responsibility was to his wife and her wellbeing in the current circumstances.

"Oh, my darling wife, we'd better get you home."

He took off his coat and wrapped it around her shoulders. He put his arm around her to lead her home.

The journey home seemed to take forever, as they both were mindful of how they must look, heads down, trying not to catch anyone's eye and hoping they wouldn't bump into one of their neighbours as they got closer to home.

Finally, they arrived at the front door. Fred pushed open the door and helped Martha into the closest chair.

"Come on, let's get your outer garments off of you and get you in bed. Then I'll call the doctor." He told her gently.

Martha looked at him silently, her face ashen, with a slight sheen of perspiration. She nodded at him, but didn't utter a word. Fred recognised that look and wanted desperately to find the right words to take the pain away. He clutched at his chest. He knew that any attempt to comfort Martha would be futile, but he wished he could give her what she wanted.

It had happened far too many times already. He took his coat from her shoulders and threw it over the nearby chair and then helped her off with her purple shawl, ribboned bonnet and matching gloves. He didn't want to leave her, so once he'd settled her into bed he ran next door and asked the young lad there to fetch the doctor.

The doctor had just finished a call in the same street so within five minutes was there, examining Martha. Once he'd cleaned himself up he returned to the living area, where Fred was stood there wringing his hands.

"I'm afraid her fears are confirmed. She's lost the baby. Just one of those things, I'm sorry to say."

Fred pinched the top of his nose as he tried to stop the pain that was washing over him. He thanked the doctor as he walked him to the door. Then as he opened the door to show the doctor out, he handed him a couple of coins in payment.

He walked slowly to the bedroom and stood at the door, summoning the strength to go in. He took a deep breath and pulled back his shoulders, before pushing open the door.

Fred looked over at his wife and smiled gently at her. He could see by her hunched shoulders and the way she was curled tightly into a ball that she had taken it rather hard. He knew she'd be blaming herself and he didn't know what he could say that would make it better.

"We can try again." He said softly, rubbing the back of his neck. .

"If only that were true." She said, her her lips trembling as she turned towards him. "But we've been married six years now and I've never managed to carry a baby more than a couple of months. There's something wrong with me. I know it."

Fred rushed over and patted his wife softly on the cheek. He sat on the edge of the bed and put his other hand on her arm.

"There's nothing you could have done. It was God's will."

Martha looked at him, but couldn't hold his gaze. He closed his eyes and rubbed his tense shoulder. *How am I going to get her to see that it's not her fault?* He thought desperately

"You should look for another wife." She told him, wetting her lips. She backed away from his touch and looked at him with a determined look in her eyes. "Someone who can give you a family."

He leant into her and brought his legs up onto the pale green marcella and cuddled up beside her on the bed. He put his arm around her waist.

"There's no one for me, except you." He said. "And if that means that we are to grow old alone, then so be it."

Martha looked at Fred with a weak smile. She had loved him ever since she'd met him when they were both nineteen.

Fred had just returned from London, where he'd gone to work for a while. He had hated it there. The amount of people crowding into such small areas. The dirt and grime everywhere, but most of all, the smog that seemed to touch everything, even the for you ate.

He'd missed the familiarity of his home town of

Bristol and was happy to be back where he belonged.

Martha had bumped into him while she was in town with her mother and sister doing some Christmas shopping. She'd noticed him across the street. His limp seeming to single him out. She remembered how handsome he'd been in his dark suit with bright red cravate.

As she'd been looking at him, he turned and caught her gaze. She'd dropped her basket in embarrassment and as she was bending down to collect the apples that were in danger of rolling into the road, he'd appeared in front of her, bending down to help her pick up her wares.

He'd smiled gently at her and then offered to help them with their bags, which they gratefully accepted. They'd bought more than they'd expected and it was starting to weigh them down.

When they reached the tram, he'd helped place all of their parcels on the floor in front of them and as he'd handed the last bag to her, he'd politely asked if he might see her again. Her mother had looked at him and then at her daughter who was so obviously smitten and smiled. She nodded and allowed him to start calling on Martha.

He'd called on her the next day, bringing a small box of chocolates with him. He'd stood at the door, fiddling with his collar and smoothing down his jacket. Martha had been equally nervous, changing outfits three times and brushing her light brown hair until it shone. She'd paced up and down the kitchen before he arrived, until her mother had gently scolded her to sit down patiently.

They'd spent the day getting to know each other and from then on had courted regularly. They'd known quite quickly how they felt about each other and had been married that next summer.

Fred was a kindly man who had gone into the cotton mill as soon as he'd left school. The owner had taken a liking to him and had offered him a promotion in his factory near London, which took the cotton from the mill and produced high quality bed linen.

Fred wasn't really an ambitious man, but out of loyalty had done as his employer had asked. He'd been thrilled when Frank had agreed for him to come back to Bristol and now he worked as an overseer in the mill. The job was harder than if he'd stayed in London, but he preferred everything about Bristol, especially after he'd met Martha.

Martha knew that Fred had always wanted a family.

Coming from a small family he'd set his heart on having a house full, but it wasn't to be. He'd suggested adoption, but Martha hated the thought of going to a baby farm. She heard so many bad things about them. There had been news of a number of procurers who'd been accused of heinous crimes concerning babies in their care, with the papers labelling them as 'angel makers'. *Even if the procurer was legit, how would they know the origins of the baby and what if they were full of disease? No,* she thought, *I'd prefer to be childless.*

She snuggled into Fred, thinking about how much she loved him. Eventually she heard the soft snores of her husband and she smiled softly. They'd get through this somehow. It was ironic that each miscarriage took a little more out of both of them, but also made them stronger together. *I just wish I could give him the child he deserves,* she thought as she finally drifted off to sleep.

CHAPTER THREE

The queue for the bathroom had been particularly long this morning. The weather was getting cooler and the children left it until the last minute to pull back the covers.

By the time Annie had got dressed, she found herself at the back of the tail of children and her heart sank as she realised she was going to be late to the dining hall. It was only gruel for breakfast today, but her grumbling tummy complained none the less.

She ran down the corridor, hoping to get in and sit down before anyone noticed, but it was not to be.

"Stop right there."

She heard the sharp voice of the matron call out. She stood rooted to the spot. Matron had never liked her, *not that she likes anyone,* Annie thought to herself as she turned to face her antagonist.

Elizabeth walked over to Annie.

"What do you think you're doing?" She asked sternly.

Annie looked down at her feet, so matron wouldn't see the fear in her eyes. She looked over at Elizabeth's feet and thought, *my, her feet are huge*, she forced her eyes slowly up to Elizabeths and noticed the hairy mole on the side of her face.

Unable to drag her eyes from it, she could feel her body shaking. She couldn't remember ever seeing Matron in a good mood. She was a tall, well built lady, who liked to use her elbows to dig into the children's sides, if they got too close.

"Going for breakfast." Annie stammered.

"You're late." Barked Elizabeth.

"I know, but there was a big queue for the bathroom this morning..."

"No excuses." Elizabeth interrupted her. "If I see you late again, you'll get the birch. Do you understand me?"

Annie nodded, eyes wide and body trembling.

Elizabeth strode off, head held high. Annie watched

her as she disappeared into the distance.

I wonder if she has any friends, she thought as she scurried down the corridor. *I've never seen her talking to anybody in a friendly manner. Not even the teachers.* She frowned as she wondered whether Mrs Price might be lonely.

Annie wasn't too far off the truth. As a girl, Elizabeth's parents had been really controlling. She hadn't been allowed to play with the other children in the neighbourhood and had never really known friendship growing up.

Her parents had been church faring people, who had strict morals, which they pressed on Elizabeth at every opportunity. They'd been busy people who hadn't really shown her any affection and so she had matured early in life.

As an adult she didn't really know how to interact with others and after a time had stopped trying. She was happiest when she saw those around her as miserable as she was.

She'd purposefully pursued the job in the workhouse, believing that being poor was a choice. If she was asked her opinion she would say that the only people who didn't have any money, were those who couldn't be bothered to work.

She had decided that she would show them the error of their ways. She made those in the workhouse work hard and if they tried to tell her that they were ill or infirm she would go out of her way to make their lives even more difficult.

As Annie reached the dining area, she gave a big sigh. Matron would often take away eating privileges so as to punish the child and they had little to eat at the best of times, so she felt relieved to have gotten away with a scolding.

She pushed open the doo and looked around. Sarah was already sat the bench, eating her gruel. She looked up and saw Annie and waved out to her friend, beckoning her to come and sit beside her. Annie got a bowl and moved over to where Sarah was sitting. She smiled as she sat down, happy to be spending time with her friend.

Sarah smiled a wide smile and while she couldn't be classed as a beautiful girl, there was something about her deep brown hair and bright blue eyes that sparkled when she was happy that somehow made her stand out in a crowd.

Her sunny disposition and willingness to stand up for

those weaker than her often made her a target of Matron's displeasure. Sarah didn't seem to mind. She'd been brought up in the workhouse and it was all she'd ever known.

They ate breakfast and chatted happily together for a few minutes, before it was time to clear up and get to their lessons.

As they walked down the long corridor to class, Sarah turned to her friend.

"You'll never guess what..." she said, then paused expectantly, waiting for Annie to suggest something.

Annie looked at her and shook her head, wrinkling her nose and furrowing her brow.

"I don't know." She said finally.

Sarah laughed.

"Okay, I'll put you out of your misery. Matron got me a job as a scullery maid."

Annie frowned. That was why Matron had been in such a good mood. She knew I was going to lose my best friend.

"Please be happy with me." Sarah begged.

Annie smiled at her.

"I am happy for you. It's great news. It's just... I'll miss you."

Sarah pouted and nodded.

I'll miss you too, but I'm twelve now. I need to get out to work."

"I know." Annie said, taking Sarah's hands in hers.

"And you'll be placed somewhere soon I expect." Sarah added.

Annie knew she couldn't be selfish. Her friend, who was always so loyal and generous needed her to be happy for her.

"Sarah, it's great news. I'm so pleased that you won't have to be working in a factory."

"Me too." Sarah said, smiling.

"Tell me all about it at lunch." Annie said, knowing they are going to be late if they didn't hurry to class.

Over dinner that evening, which consisted of a thin broth and a small chunk of bread, Sarah told Annie a little bit more about the job.

"It's for a family who live on the edge of Bristol. I'll be expected to scrub floors, empty the ashes from the fire and that sort of thing. The main thing is that I'll finally have money of my own."

Annie watched her friend chattering excitedly about the job. Although Sarah had been sent out occasionally to work in the nearby factories, she didn't really know about life outside the workhouse. Getting this job not only meant that she'd earn her own wages, but she'd finally have some freedom, so this was a great opportunity for her.

"So when do you go?" Annie said, once Sarah had told her everything.

"Oh, not until next week. We've got plenty of time."

"What will I do without you?" Annie lamented.

"Don't worry. I'll come and visit you whenever I can. Maybe we could sneak out and take a walk or something."

Annie nodded happily. She felt a large weight fall from her shoulders as she realised her friend wasn't going to desert her.

For Annie, the week seemed to fly by. Before she knew it, Sarah was sat on the edge of her bed with a pillowcase filled with her belongings set down beside her feet.

Matron was stood over her, looking at her fob watch

watch with narrowed eyes.

"Come along." Elizabeth said. "Better not be late."

Sarah nodded and stood up. Chewing her lip, she turned to Annie and gave her a quick hug before stepping to the side of the matron.

"I'll be back as soon as possible." She said to Annie.

"You promise?" Replied Annie.

"Of course, you're my best friend. I can't lose you."

Matron grinned sardonically. She doubted the two of them would ever see each other again and she was pleased that she was instrumental in breaking up their friendship. *I've never had a friend and I've turned out all right,* she thought smugly, not realising how much richer her life could have been.

Annie watched as Sarah walked off with Elizabeth, ready to start her new life. She looks so small next to Matron, she thought as a lone tear crept down her cheek.

CHAPTER FOUR

"Put the kettle on love." Flora shouted to Martha, as she pushed open the door.

Martha looked up from her ironing in delight. She loved her family dearly, but her smile widened just a little more when she saw her sister brought her niece to visit.

"Hello you two." She said, as she put the iron down on the stove, careful to make sure that it faced inwards. It was still hot and she was worried in case Daisy stumbled nearby.

Daisy ran to Martha and gave her a huge hug.

"Auntie." She said enthusiastically.

"Hello, my darling niece." She said returning the hug just as eagerly. Daisy was a cheerful child and never failed to put a smile on her face.

She breathed a deep sigh of contentment as she tipped a little tea into the pot. Picking the kettle up from above the stove, she poured some water into the pot. She gave it a quick stir, before mashing it against the sides of the pot. Taking it over to the table, where Flora had already made herself comfortable, she went back for the cups.

"Now Daisy, are you hungry?" She asked, looking fondly at her niece who'd been staring out the window.

Daisy nodded, giggling at something she'd spotted out of the window.

"I'll get you some bread and jam then. Now sit yourself at the table."

Daisy dragged herself away from the window and pulled herself up onto the table . She sat there with her head in her hands, squeezing her cheeks together, trying to make the adults laugh.

"Elbows off the table." Flora said sternly, trying not to laugh at her precocious child.

Martha brought over the cups and a plate with a small chunk of bread and jam and sat down opposite her sister.

"So what do I owe the pleasure?" She asked smiling at Flora.

Her sister looked at her with raised her eyebrows and tilted her head to the side.

"Can't a lady visit her sister?" Flora said smiling disingenuously.

"Yes, but I wasn't expecting you until the end of the week." Martha teased, smirking at her sister. They saw each other at least one once a week. She always looked forward to the visit, but they normally saw each other on a Friday and it was only Tuesday.

She looked at her sister skeptically, knowing there was a favour she was going to ask. Flora laughed and leant back in her chair.

"Well I was wondering if you minded having Daisy for a couple of hours while I go shopping? We've been invited out this evening and I need a new dress. And it's just easier to do it without Daisy being there."

"Of course." Laughed Martha. "You know I always love to have my niece. You've just got to ask. I've got some paper and a crayon. I'll sit her down here at the table and she can she can make you a picture for when you get back."

"Thank you." Said Flora, waving her hand in the air. "But tea first, and you can tell me how you are after last week." She asked in a quieter voice.

Martha's smile faded a little.

She busied herself pouring the tea and then sat down with her cup against her lips, trying to steady the emotions that welled up inside her.

"It's okay, you know." Said Flora softly.

"I know, but I know how much Fred wants children, and for him to have to go through this rigmarole again, I'm heartbroken."

Flora thought for a moment, before bringing up the subject.

"What about going to one of those procurers?" She asked.

Martha looked up sharply. Flora knew how she felt about the baby farmers, so she couldn't believe that she'd mentioned it again.

"They're not all bad." Flora reminded her.

"But some of them are evil and riddled with germs. I agree with government. They should all be banned.

"But what would happen to the babies?" Flora asked

gently.

Martha sat there deep in thought.

"I wouldn't mind adopting." She said finally. "I just don't like the thought of those evil people, who pretend to help, but do it just for the money. It should be properly regulated."

Flora nodded in agreement, patting her sister on the arm as she did so.

"All I've ever wanted to be as a wife and mother" Annie said sadly.

"I wish it could be different for you." Flora said. "I know you'd make a good mother, after all, look how you are with Daisy?"

"Well if it's not meant to be, it's not meant to be." Martha said, crossing her arms over her chest.

Flora could see that her sister didn't want to discuss it any further.

"You've always got Daisy." Flora reminded her. "I'll let you borrow her anytime you like." She said gently before changing the subject

They supped their tea, before Flora stood up and took her leave. She bent down to Daisy, who'd decided the rug in front of the stove was the best place to start drawing.

Martha was glad that she'd had the forethought to make sure the iron was turned away. She didn't know what she'd do, if she was the cause of anything happening to her precious niece.

"You be good for your aunt." Flora said, tapping her daughter gently on the shoulder..

"Yes mama." Daisy said obediently, giving her mum a quick peck on the cheek, before returning to her drawing.

The two sisters laughed.

"She'll be fine. Take your time." Martha told her sister as she opened the door for her.

"I know." Flora replied, as she scampered down the steps and turned towards town.

Martha went back to her ironing, watching Daisy as she sat with her tongue out the side of her mouth in concentration. She loved looking after her niece, even if sometimes it did remind her of what she couldn't have for herself.

CHAPTER FIVE

Every weekend Annie would look out of the gates expectantly, waiting for Sarah to arrive as promised.

Standing there for ages looking out at the passerby, she would getting a sinking feeling in the pit of her stomach as he would realise once again that Sarah wasn't going to make an appearance.

Sarah had been distraught when she'd realised that her new position was going to at her employer's countryside property in Gloucestershire.

Realising that she'd be unable to return to the workhouse as promised, she'd hoped that she'd have a chance to let Annie know. But just two days later they'd packed up and gone and there had been nothing she could do.

I wish I could have found a way of getting word to her before I left, Sarah thought despondently, *I hope she can forgive me. I'll tell her how sorry I am, if I see her again.*

Annie eventually gave up on Sarah coming back to her. *Why would she lie?* She thought. *I thought she was my friend. Did I mean so little to her?* Once she realised that she was on her own again, she became quite forlorn.

The crowd that had bullied her before had continued as soon as they saw Sarah disappearing out of the gates, and Annie felt that she was totally alone.

The pushing and shoving had turned to pinches and punches, but they were sneaky with it, and Annie always seemed to get caught by the teacher, when she retaliated.

The teacher could see how unhappy Annie was and would often give her the benefit of the doubt, but if Matron were to catch her fighting, she knew she was in for a beating.

The bullies quickly realised this and determined to heap as much cruelty on her as possible, made sure that they provoked her in matron's presence at every opportunity.

After a particularly cruel flogging Annie led in her bed sobbing, holding one hand in the other. They were both throbbing from being slapped raw, but the pain in one of them travelled the length of her arm and felt as if it were never going to stop. *I can't go on like this*, she thought.

"Are you all right?" She heard someone stood over her whisper.

She looked up and wiped the tears from her eyes. It was her teacher. She sat up and nodded hesitantly.

"Let me see." Hilda said gently.

Annie held out her hand and showed Hilda the red welts on her hands.

"Oh you poor thing." The teacher said, putting a little balm on Annie's palms.

Hilda looked around covertly. If Matron were to find out she'd been here, she knew that she'd accuse her of being disrespectful to the workhouse regulations.

"Try to get some sleep." She said quietly as she stood up and crept back out into the corridor.

Annie smiled sadly at the kindness of the teacher,

but knew another beating was just around the corner. *I'm going to have to leave and find a job of my own,* she decided, as she started thinking about escaping.

Her opportunity came a few days later. She was told by matron that the next day she would have to get up extra early as she was expected to go with a few of the other children to do some work for a nearby business owner. *I'll put as many of my clothes on as possible and then find a way of sneaking away before it's time to return,* she thought.

She tossed and turned throughout the night, worrying that someone was going to be able to read her thoughts and stop her from leaving. She got up before anyone else stirred and started layering up her clothes, without looking too suspicious.

Once she'd got dressed, she lay back down, sick with fear. She was certain that someone would find out her plan and tell the matron. Annie knew that if she were aware of Annie's plans, she'd not only stop Annie from leaving, but would also give her a good hiding. *I need to act normal*, she thought as she tried to stop her hands from trembling.

Once it was time for breakfast, she made her way quietly into the hall and tried to eat her gruel as quickly as possible. Sick with nerves she left most of it congealing in the bottom of the bowl. Knowing that she wanted to avoid the bullies, she sat in a far corner, waiting until it was time for them to be called to leave.

She couldn't believe it when she was finally outside the workhouse gates. She took a deep breath, before getting in the cart with the other children.

Her eyes darted everywhere, watching the world go by as the horse pulled them closer to Bristol town centre. The town began to become more built up, with shops and factories dotted along the streets.

I'm sure I'll be able to find work and somewhere to stay here, she thought as the fear started to turn to excitement.

The cart stopped outside a huge building. Annie looked at it in awe. The red bricked walls and turrets either side of a large arched dome stood high above her and the black wrought iron gates stood oppressively before her.

Then she reminded herself that she wasn't actually going to go in. This was her best chance of getting away, so she looked around her to see if anyone was paying her any attention, but everyone was jostling each other, talking over one another, apprehensive of what was

was expected of them.

Most of them spent their time shut up in the workhouse, so getting out was an adventure in itself, even if it did mean they would have a hard days graft to do.

"Come on, get down from there." The driver's voice boomed out.

The children started clambering down and Annie held back so that she wouldn't get entangle in the small group stepping through the gates.

The driver started leading the children in to meet the factory owner, and Annie saw her chance. She swiftly ran behind a carriage that was parked against the pavement and hid watching as the group from the workhouse disappeared inside the gates.

She waited until the driver returned to the cart and without as much as a glance in her direction he flicked his whip and the horse started trotting away from the building. Annie breathed a sigh of relief and looked around. She was free to start her new life.

CHAPTER SIX

Annie watched as a number of people all seemed to be heading in the same direction and decided to follow them.

They seem to know where to go, she reasoned as only a ten year old can do. She walked slowly down the road, looking around in amazement at all the different buildings that lined the pavement. They seemed to lean down towards her, beckoning her in.

She'd never seen a church before and when she came upon the tall gothic building she couldn't help but stand there, mouth wide open in wonderment at the church spires.

Finally she found herself in what seemed to be a shopping area. She looked around at canopies that covered the shop windows and the costermongers, with their small carts and baskets.

This is it, she thought. *I'm bound to find work here.* Her nose twitched with the delicious aromas around her and found her mouth watering. There was a fishmongers, butchers, bakery. The smell of the bread, mingling with the fresh smell of coffee was something she'd never experienced before.

As she stood there looking around, mouth wide open and staring unabashedly around her, she found herself being jostled by the crowds of passersby.

The deafening cacophony around her made her head ache. As she looked up it seemed that the buildings were falling towards her. She felt butterflies in the pit of her stomach. She took a step back.

"Oy. Mind where you're going." A gruff voice said.

"Sorry, sir." She replied nervously and backed away, knocking into someone else as she did so.

She stopped and took a deep breath, feeling overwhelmed with the amount of activity going on around her. The people treated her as though she were invisible as they went about their daily lives. Eventually she decided that she needed to move to somewhere quieter to gather her thoughts.

Annie really only remembered life in the workhouse, and it had been located in the suburbs. Life had seemed much quieter there, especially as she spent most of her life inside.

Not knowing where to start she started to back away from the crowds until she found the cold stone of a nearby shop behind her. She slumped against it and looked at the traffic that was carrying people around. *What's that? It looks a little like a cart, but covered in, and bigger. I've never seen something so strange?* She thought flabbergasted at the sight of the horse drawn tram that was carrying people around the town centre.

Shivering and stomach rumbling, she decided she needed to start looking for work and somewhere to stay. Looking out at the bewildering sights in front of her she wasn't quite sure where to start. She pushed herself away from the wall and started walking to her left, watching her step to avoid the debris that lingered on the streets.

She reached a small alleyway, and wondered if she might have better luck in finding someone to take her in where it was a little quieter.

As she was wandering up the alley, wondering what

to do next, she saw a group of children near the end of the passageway and grinned in delight. *They'll be able to tell me where I can get some food and somewhere to stay.* She thought expectantly

She approached the gang and smiled at them.

"Hello." she said, holding her arms behind her back and straightening her shoulders.

"What do you want?" The biggest of the group said sharply, moving closer to her until he was towering above her.

Annie backed away slightly scared of the reaction from the young boy, who reminded her of the bullies back at the workhouse.

"I need some help. I've just ran away from the workhouse and I don't know what to do or where to go. Can you help me?" She pleaded

"Why should we?" He replied gruffly. "We ain't got enough ourselves, what makes you think we would want to help you?"

Annie blinked at him, not knowing what else to say, but not quite ready to give up.

"Do you know where I might get some work?" She asked keeping her fingers crossed that he wouldn't see how nervous she really was.

Another of the boys moved forwards from the group and with his chest puffed up and his chin held high, he stared at her.

"Din't you 'ear what 'e said?" He growled. "We ain't got nothing and we don't know nothing. Now get, before we take that nice shawl you got round your shoulders, and its a good job those shoes are too small..."

Annie backed away, swallowing hard. The boy took a step towards her and she turned and fled as quickly as she could. As she looked over her shoulder to make sure they weren't giving chase, she noticed one of them going to go after her, but the boy that had spoken first put his arm in the way to stop him.

"Leave it, we don't need any more trouble, we already got enough as it is." She heard him say as they turned away from her. She continued to run to the entrance of the alleyway and ran straight into a woman, knocking her basket out of her hand.

"I'm sorry, ma'am." She said, cheeks turning the same colour red as the nearby pillar box. She knelt down quickly and grabbing frantically, picked up the apples and put them back in the basket. She handed the basket back to its owner, apologising once more.

The woman snatched the basket and looked, mealy mouthed, down her nose at her. She hurummped before flouncing off, leaving Annie hands on her knees, trying to catch her breath.

Annie covered her mouth with her hand. She took a deep inhale. *What if I've done the wrong thing?* she thought. She'd been so excited about leaving the workhouse, and the bullying.

Now that she was here in the town, she realised that she hadn't really thought through what she was going to do now she was here.

She chewed her lip as she tried to establish what to do next. She decided to ask someone where she was and see if she recognised the name. *If it isn't too faraway, maybe I could walk back to the workhouse, say I got lost,* she thought hopefully.

"Excuse me." She said hesitantly to the first person she saw walking down the street.

The man brushed past her as though she wasn't there.

"Excuse me." She said again, a little more loudly to the person heading towards her.

Again, the woman put her head down and just ignored her.

Annie frowned. She could feel the acid rising in her chest and her palms sweating. *I need to do something, but everyone seems so unfriendly*, she thought. *Maybe they're just busy. Maybe that one selling vegetables might be able to tell me what direction I need to go.*

"Excuse me." She said as confidently as she could muster.

The man peered out of the door and saw the little girl looking up at him.

"What can I do for you, me love?" He asked kindly.

Annie gave a sigh of relief.

"Where are we?" She asked

"We be in Wesleyfield.' He replied, scratching his head and staring at her suspiciously.

"Would you be able to tell me the way to the workhouse?" she asked politely.

The man rubbed his chin in thought.

"Why do you want to be going there?" He asked puzzled that anyone would willingly take themselves off to that god forsaken place.

"Well, you see, I ran away, but I think I might have made a mistake." She confessed.

"I don't know exactly where it is. I know it's that way. Why don't you ask a policeman, they might know." He suggested.

Annie thanked him and turned in the direction he'd pointed.She saw a big burly man dressed in his uniform with long ginger whiskers. She looked down to where his hand was resting on his truncheon and shivered. *I can't ask a policeman*, she thought. *He might lock me away from running away.*

By this time it was getting dusky and Annie was worried that she'd get lost trying to find her way back. *Best to wait until morning*, she decided, as her eyes darted up and down the street, trying to find somewhere she might be able to stay until dawn.

Some of the buildings seemed to be built over the pavements, being held up by stilts. *I don't know how that works,* she thought. *I hope they don't fall on me.* The gas lighting was starting to come on and they cast a warm glow on the buildings that towered over the narrow pathways.

Noticing another alleyway, she decided that now the shops were closing that she might be able to find shelter in one of the doorways. Her stomach rumbled loudly. *I wish I had some way of getting some food*, she fretted, putting her hand over her stomach as if to comfort it .

She sat down on a small step outside the pawn shop. It was a small doorway with a large sign overhead, which swung in the breeze. She looked through the lead lined window. She could see a variety of things, from kitchen utensils and clothes, through to brooches and pocket watches.

She frowned, wondering what sort of shop it might be and shivered, as the night started to fall around her. She pulled her shawl tightly round her, hunching her shoulders as she did so. She tucked her feet under her body, remembering what the boy had said earlier about taking her shoes and shut her eyes.

As she did so, she could hear the noises of the canopies over the shops being wound in and the doors being locked up for the night.

Annie could hear the sound of people milling around on their way home to their homes. Thinking she was going to get attacked by a gang of lads, or the rats that she could hear scurrying around her, Annie shivered.

As darkness fell, the noises grew quieter, but all Annie could hear were the unfamiliar sounds of the nocturnal animals. Although her eyelids were heavy, she found herself unable to surrender to the sleep her young body desperately needed.

CHAPTER SEVEN

As dusk broke, Annie sat up. She felt exhausted. Her stomach grumbled loudly and she put her hand over her stomach and stretched her stiff body, feeling every ache and pain as she did so.

She hadn't eaten since the previous morning, and desperately needed something. She decided to get up from the step and take a look around the market, to see if there were any scraps left over from the previous day.

She was surprised to see that it was already busy with the shopkeepers, who were setting up for that day's business. *Maybe one of them need a hand,* she thought. *They might give me some food in return for labour.*

She walked hesitantly to the first shop and asked if he needed some help, but he abruptly rebuffed her. Unwilling to give up at the first hurdle, Annie took a deep breath before moving on to the next one.

An hour later she sat down on the kerb of the cobbled street, cold and exhausted. She held her head in her hands, trying to think of how she could get herself out of the mess she found herself in.

She could feel the tears in the back of her head, and they made her nose hurt. Her shoulders felt as though the weight of the world was upon them and she wan't sure if she had the strength to stand back up.

Everyone she had approached had sent her away with a flea in her ear. They already had enough difficulty putting food on the table as it was, they couldn't afford to worry about some little slip of a girl.

She thought about taking a slice of bread, off one of the stalls, but was too scared. She'd heard horror stories of children being sent to prison for stealing and so she decided that she'd rather starve than to be in prison.

Matron had told the children of the pie-poudre or piepowder court. Coming from the French 'pieds poudrés' which is roughly translated as dusty feet, these courts had been set up in Norman times , and were held on market days to deal with the scallywags who visited on trading days for the sole purpose of stealing.

If the children did anything that Matron thought unruly or naughty she would threaten the children with the pie-poudre. Annie had had many a nightmare about being sent there.

She wondered if she might be close to the court and shivered suddenly at the thought. *If I get caught stealing they'll drag me there kicking and screaming,* she fretted.

She wasn't to know the pie-poudre only existed to prosecute visitors to the area, when a quick decision would have to be made. She'd have been more likely to have been sent to a reformatory school as her punishment.

While Annie had been trying to find work amongst the shopkeepers, the streets had gotten busier. She looked around in amazement as somebody banged into her, and as she moved back, she was jostled again.

The smell of horse manure and chemicals mixed with the more pleasurable smells of food and beverages was starting to make her feel sick. *I need to start moving towards the workhouse again,* she thought as she turned in a circle, trying to get her sense of direction once more.

She decided that she would cross the street to the other side, which looked a little quieter. She looked both ways before stepping off of the kerb, not seeing the tram that was coming towards her.

She gasped as an arm reached out and pulled her back. She stumbled backwards and fell to the floor. As she sat back up, she saw the back of the tram. *I would have been hit by that if someone hadn't pulled me back,* she thought, eyes wide open with fear.

Annie looked behind her to see her saviour. An elderly lady smiled at her.

"Are you all right?" She asked.

Annie looked up at her through her long eyelashes. The lady looked kindly, with white hair that sparkled in the sun and a ruddy complexion, Annie felt a sense of calmness and nodded with a hesitant smile.

"I'm sorry, ma'am. It's just so busy here. I'm just not used to it. What is that contraption anyway?"

The lady laughed at her as she helped Annie up.

"Hello. My name is Ida and that there is a tram. It's a horse-drawn sort of bus which takes people in and out of town. That one there comes from Kingswood, goes into the centre and then on to Ashton Gate, I believe.

"Never took one myself. Too dangerous. The roads have become much busier since they've been introduced. Accident waiting to happen in my opinion, especially on this road. It's so wide." Her voice rising as she rallied about the dangers of these new-fangled vehicles.

"Oh." Annie said, not sure how to react to what Ida had just told her.

"And you are?" Ida asked expectantly.

Annie blushed beetroot as she realised she hadn't told Ida her name.

"I'm Annie. How do you do." She said politely, holding out her hand.

Ida laughed softly.

"No need for such formality here." She said.

Anne blushed even deeper and put her hand down by her side.

"May I asked where you're from if you've never seen the tram before?" Ida asked.

Annie started to tell her, when Ida interrupted.

"Sounds like quite a tale. Maybe we should find somewhere to sit down before you continue. I'm not as young as I once was." Ida said smiling and putting her hand on her back as if it emphasis the point.

They sat down on a nearby bench and Annie turned her body to face Ida before continuing her story.

"So what are your plans now?" Ida asked.

"I was trying to get back to the workhouse, I've made such a mistake." Admitted Annie.

Ida recoiled in shock.

"You can't go back. Not after what you've just told me. You'd never survive the beating that the matron would give you for disappearing in the first place."

Annie's jaw dropped. She hadn't even thought of the consequences of going back to the workhouse, but she shuddered as she realised that what Ida had just said rang true.

"So what should I do?" She asked. "I can't live on the streets. I found that out last night. I'll starve if I don't find somewhere to go soon. What choice do I have?"

Ida screwed up her nose and pursed her lips.

"Well, my son works in a factory, just over there." She said pointing over Annie's shoulder.

"What sort of factory?" Annie asked. "Would they

give me a job? She asked hopefully.

Ida smiled sympathetically, but shook her head.

"I don't expect so, not if you just turned up out of the blue, but I'm thinking you could sneak in there at night for shelter. You might even find some scraps if you're lucky. Better than being out 'ere. I'm just sorry I can't take you in. We haven't got the money or the space, you see."

Annie thought for a moment. A roof over her head would be a start. *I don't think I could spend another night out here, with all those weird noises,* she thought.

"And maybe, if you were there in the day, you could find yourself some work, with the other children, cleaning out underneath the machinery. My son says there's loads of children that work there. They might not even notice you."

Annie nodded, feeling more hopeful l than she had since she'd arrived in the town centre.

"If I prove to them that I'm hard working maybe someone will give me a penny, then I could buy myself some food." She said hopefully.

Ida looked over at the young girl. *She seems such a nice young soul. I hope it turns out all right for her*, she thought.

"But don't tell anyone I sent you. And definitely don't let any of the bosses catch you there." She warned. "If they knew you were sleeping there, I'm not sure what they would do. At least it'll be warmer there and from memory of when I worked in a factory, there's lots of nooks and crannies you can hide in."

Annie promised she wouldn't tell anyone that Ida had suggested she go there and with that Ida stood up, patting Annie softly on the hand. Annie looked down at the elderly hand with paper thin skin and brown age spots. *I don't want her to leave me on my own*, she thought sadly.

"Good luck Annie. I hope you find your true path." Ida said gently as she set off.

"Thank you." Annie responded gratefully, watching Ida disappear into the crowd.

She spent the day roaming the streets, searching for scraps. She managed to find a hunk of dried bread and bit down on it hungrily. Chewing the bread until it was soft enough to swallow, Annie thought about how lucky she'd been in meeting Ida. *And not only cos she saved me from being flattened by that big monster*, she thought.

As dusk started to fall, Annie began to feel quite excited about getting off the street, not realising that her next step on the journey would lead her to some dangerous working conditions.

CHAPTER EIGHT

Annie followed the directions that Ida gave her and soon found herself in front of another big factory.

It was similar to the one she'd meant to start work in a couple of days before, and she felt a nervous bubbling in her stomach, taking in the soot lined red brick and lead lined windows in front of her.

She stood for a moment looking at the men spilling out of the factory gates. They were all dressed similarly, with white collars and dark suits. They were laughing and joking as they wandered off down the road from the factory. The women followed soon after and were quieter and looked like they could fall over at a moments notice.

I'm going to have to find another way in, she thought. She waited until the place seemed empty and then started to creep around the building looking for a small space she could fit through.

"What do you think you're doing?

She heard a gruff voice behind her.

Annie turned quickly, petrified that she'd been caught by one of bosses that Ida had warned her about.

She looked up at a broad man, with dirty blond hair, ruddy cheeks and a suspicious look in his pale grey eyes.

"Please sir, I'm sorry. It's just that I need some work and somewhere to sleep. I'm so cold and so hungry."

John looked down at the scrawny little girl in front of him. She was a sorry sight, but he knew he couldn't be to lenient or he might get taken as a fool.

"Where's your parents? Shouldn't they be looking after you?" He asked a little softer.

"I ain't got no parents sir. They're both dead," she said, telling a white lie as she didn't know whether or not her father was still alive.

John felt a sadness within him. He had a brood of seven at home, and hated the thought that they might one day be left alone to fend for themselves.

"So where have you come from?" He asked, thinking that she didn't look like the usual street urchins he saw roaming the streets. She seemed cleaner and more polite than the orphaned children who ran amok around town.

"The workhouse sir. I was getting picked on, and Matron, she would beat me, even though it weren't my fault. I'm ran away two days ago and haven't eaten since then, well, except for a small chunk of bread I found on the floor."

John frowned. He still wasn't sure what he should do with her. There was no question of him taking her back home with him. They didn't have enough to eat as it was. *Those boys seem to have bottomless pits*, he thought.

"So what were you doing when I caught you? You looked like you were trying to break in."

"I was, sir." She admitted. "Someone said that maybe I could find sleep here tonight and tomorrow help the other children clean under the machinery."

"Who told you that?" He asked.

"I couldn't possibly say. You see, I made a promise." She replied.

John put his hand to his chin, rubbing his finger up and down in thought.

"Okay. I can't give you no food, but I can give you some shelter, I suppose. I'll show you a way in, but if you get found out I had nothing to do with it." He said sternly.

"No, of course not. I wouldn't tell nobody" She said. "Thank you so much"

John walked her round to the edge of the factory and showed her a door, which was quite hidden from public site.

"Go in there.If you turn to your right and go a few feet, you'll find a warm spot to sleep. Now remember, keep out of sight and I'll come and find you in the morning."

Annie nodded and as she cautiously pulled the door to her she turned to thank John.

Tomorrow, I'll show you a job you can do, make yourself useful. There's lots of children cleaning under the machinery, so one more won't be noticed." He said as he turned to leave.

Annie followed John's instructions and was delighted to feel the warmth from the pipes that ran above her head. Feeling relieved that she was out from the streets, she lay down, pulling her shawl over her like a blanket.

She thought about what had happened in the short space of time since she'd left the workhouse. *If I'd known how scary it was out on the streets I'd never been brave enough to leave. At least here I can sleep,* she thought, finally feeling safer than she had since she'd left the workhouse. Within minutes. She'd fallen asleep, starving and exhausted and hopeful for the next day.

CHAPTER NINE

The next day, Annie woke early. She felt more positive than she had since she'd left the workhouse, but still nervous that she was going to get caught. She pushed herself as far back as she could, as she heard footsteps coming towards her.

"Annie." She heard a voice whisper above her.

She recognised it as John and stepped out from her hiding place.

"There you are." He said, as he gave her a nubbin of bread spread thinly with a little jam.

"This 'ere is Thomas." He said, as he pulled Thomas in front of him. "He's going to show you what to do, and if you're good, I'll try and find something else for you to eat later on.

Annie nodded as she devoured the bit of bread, swallowing hungrily. Thomas watched her silently, eyebrows raised as she polished off the slice in no time at all. He was younger than Annie, and slightly smaller. With a dark mop of hair and mischievous blue eyes, Annie couldn't help smile at him.

Thomas smiled back and Annie felt as though she'd found a kindred spirit.

John stood over her and said sternly, "And if anyone asks who you are, just say you're new and shrug a bit, then try to get away from them as soon as possible. Do you think you can do that?" he asked.

Annie nodded, lifting her shoulders to her ears in a deep shrug.

John could help the belly laugh, as he struggled to maintain an air of authority.

"I'm being serious. If anyone finds out about you, you'll have to leave and if they find out I've helped you, I'll be out of 'ere too."

Annie looked at him with wide eyes and nodded earnestly. She didn't want to leave and so she would do anything to make sure her secret was safe.

"Come on then. Thomas is going to show you what

to do."

Annie followed Thomas into one of the large production areas and watched solemnly as he showed her the machines.

"When you go over, grab the cotton, but be careful mind, the machines are still working, so they can be dangerous. If you lift your head up too high, they'll knock your block off." He told her.

She looked at him nervously.

Don't worry, it's not dangerous, as long as you do what I tell you." He said confidently.

As they entered the production area Annie wanted to put her hands over her ears. She wasn't sure how anyone could hear each other above the rattle and hiss of the machinery. The air was hot and dusty and Annie felt like she had trouble breathing.

Annie worked alongside Thomas all day and as everyone was getting ready to leave John bought a little scrap of food and told her to go and hide in her place before anybody noticed. She crept away, making sure she wasn't seen and hungrily wolfed down the food that John had given her. She settled down to sleep, exhausted from the days work, but feeling a contentment she'd never felt before.

The next few weeks followed a similar pattern and Annie and Thomas became close friends. They looked out for each other and chatted as they crawled under the machines, pulling out the cotton and cleaning underneath.

Occasionally John would slip her a penny and during the weekend she'd sneak out of the factory and make her way to the market, just to have a look around, and enjoy the different noises and smells of the stalls. She felt a sense of freedom and independence that the workhouse had never been able to provide.

CHAPTER TEN

Fred pushed open the door to Frank's office and poked his head in.

"Good morning Sir." Fred said.

"Good morning Fred, so what do I owe the pleasure of your company?" His boss said gesturing him to come in and sit down.

Fred sat down and squirmed slightly, trying to get comfortable. Even though he got on well with Frank, he still felt nervous going into the office to discuss work matters.

"I thought perhaps that we should talk about the new welfare reforms."

Frank nodded, putting his fingers together in a

steeple as he looked expectantly at Fred.

"Go on."

"I've been thinking about some health and safety measures we could implement." He said, hoping his boss was in a good mood.

"And how much are they going to cost?" Frank asked, raising his eyebrows.

Fred gulped. He knew that they were going to cost more than Frank would be willing to pay out, unless someone could prove it would have a good return on investment.

"Well Sir, It wouldn't cost much to implement, not really. You see, it's to do with the young children that go underneath the machines to keep them clean throughout the day."

"Yes?" Frank replied, raising his shoulders in an off hand manner.

"Well, it can be quite dangerous for them to go under the machine while they're still moving. I think that we should wait until the machines are turned off."

"But we've taught them to be careful, haven't we?" asked Frank. It wasn't that he was an uncaring man. He did his best for his workers, but he was also pragmatic about his business. If he didn't keep up with the competition, then his customers would go elsewhere, and they'd all be out of job.

"Yes, Sir. But shouldn't we be looking at ways in which to make operations safer, if we can?"

"Yes but not at any cost. If we lose business then they wouldn't have any work. That would be a problem for them surely?"

"Yes, of course. But I was wondering that if the children cleaned the machines during the tea breaks and during lunchtime then it wouldn't really affect productivity."

"When would they have their break?" Frank asked.

"When everyone goes back to work after their break. They don't have as long a break anyway."

"And will the machines stay clean enough? Frank queried.

"I believe so, sir, but we could maybe do a trial and see?" Fred asked hopefully.

Frank sat back in his large leather chair, his hand stroking his chin.

After a moments contemplation he said, "Maybe it could work. Let me ever think about it for a few days and I'll come back to you."

Fred nodded. "It would show them that we are serious about the new reforms and about improving their working conditions.

"Yes, but we can't do anything that will affect our profits." Warned Frank as he waved Fred away.

"Leave it with me and I'll give you my decision." He told him.

Fred nodded and stood up. He looked around at the office, with the big desk, large leather chair and mahogany coving. He knew that his boss had certain standards to maintain but sometimes he wondered if Frank's priorities might be a little skewed.

"Thank you for your time sir." He said as he turned to leave.

"Good bye Fred." Frank said, as he bowed his head over the paperwork on his desk.

As he was walking down the corridor back to work he couldn't get rid of a small niggle in the back of his head, telling that he should have pushed the conversation a little bit more. As he reached the shop floor one of his men turned to him.

"All right Fred?" Albert asked, noticing that Fred

looked worried about something.

"Yes, Albert. Everything fine. Just been to see the gov'er." Fred told him, knowing he would need no further explanation.

"Oh." Replied Albert shrugging, as he turned back round to continue working.

It wasn't that the workers didn't like the boss, its just that there had always been and always would be a them and us attitude between management and the workers. *Luckily they seem me as one of them*, thought Fred as he went about his duties.

Throughout the day, he couldn't shake the feeling that something was going to go wrong.

CHAPTER ELEVEN

Annie was working as usual, sweeping the floor, while Thomas crawled under the machine to pull out the cotton that had started to build up behind it. As he backed out a sudden noise alarmed him and he turned quickly to find out what it was.

"Careful." Shouted Annie, but it was too late. She watched in horror as Thomas fell to the floor.

Annie screamed and went to run towards him, but one of the men pull her back.

"Stay here. That's not a place for a young lass like you."

Annie stood frozen to the spot as she saw a pool of blood spread from under Thomas. She knew he was dead, but couldn't help moving macabrely towards him to get a closer look to make sure.

John saw her moving towards the body and pulled her away, telling her to get back, but she couldn't move. She stood there, hands over her eyes, unable to cry.

"Annie, come here. Are you okay?" He asked as he put his arm around her.

She nodded silently and pulled away, devastated that she has lost another friend.

John knew that Fred would be looking around, making sure he knew exactly who was there, and if he happened upon Annie, he might wonder who she was.

"Come on, we'll get you back to your corner." He told her.

Annie found it hard to turn her head away from the blood, but John was a big man and put his arm around her shoulders and led her away.

He took her shawl and wrapped it around her shoulders, telling her to stay there until the next day, once things had settle down. Annie nodded, but John could tell by her glazed eyes that she wasn't thinking straight. He wanted to stay and comfort the young girl, but knew he had to get back to the machine room before anyone noticed him missing.

Annie sat there shaking her head, trying to rid herself of her thoughts, but unable to stop the feeling of being curse. *Why does everyone I love leave me*, she thought desperately.

Each time she closed her eyes to try and get some sleep, she could see the accident unfold again, making her feel sick to her stomach.

Exhausted her body finally gave in and she fell into a troubled sleep, haunted by the sight of Thomas's pale lifeless body as he lay there, the pool of blood spooling from under him.

She woke sobbing, as she remembered the events of the day before. She wasn't sure if she could face going back to the machines and seeing the spot where Thomas had fallen. *But if I don't work, then John won't give me any food. I don't know that I've got a choice,* she thought miserably.

Fred had also had trouble sleeping. He felt a great weight on his shoulders. He knew Thomas's parents personally and had gone on ahead of the lad who had carried Thomas back home to tell them of the devastating news.

He'd trudged down the hill to where the worker's cottages stood and hesitated before knocking heavily on the door. He'd watched as the light went out of their eyes as the realisation of what Fred had told them hit them both.

Not only had they lost their son, but they'd also lost Thomas's wages which had helped put food on the table for the rest of family. He turned silently, leaving the cottage, while Joe had put his arm around his wife and pulled her to him. The other children looking up at them, not quite knowing what was going on.

When he got home and told Martha what had happened, she had tried to tell him that he'd done his best. Still he couldn't help feeling guilty that he'd not done more to prevent the accident occurring.

He'd known that he should have pushed Frank harder the other day, insisted that the machines stop before the children climbed underneath, rather than nod mutely as his boss had told him he'd think about it.

CHAPTER TWELVE

A week after the accident, Fred was still feeling guilty. As much as Martha tried to tell him that it wasn't his responsibility, Fred knew in his heart that every time he saw Thomas's parents, he would feel he should have put his case much stronger to the cotton mill owner.

Lying in bed she wrapped her arms around her husband to comfort him, Martha felt a strong pain rip through her stomach. She put her hands to her nightgown and knew straight away what had just happened. She let out a loud sob.

"What's wrong?" Fred asked anxiously.

Martha climbed quickly out of bed, looking for some rags to soak up the bleeding.

Fred realised what was going on, grabbed some towels and helped her back into bed.

"Are you okay?" He asked.

"I can't do this again." She told him. "I know it should get easier, but I can't face losing another one."

Fred nodded sadly.

"I'll go round first thing and see the doctor. Get him to make sure you're all right." He told her, as he cuddled into her.

Martha turned her back and closed her eyes tightly. Fred waited for her to sleep and then crept out of bed unable to stop his thoughts from invading his peace. He went into the kitchen and sat close to the stove that was still giving off a little heat. He picked up his pipe tapped on the stove's edge, before filling it and lighting it. He rarely indulged, but on occasions as this one, he liked the comfort sucking on the pipe gave him.

He sat there for a time mulling things over. It seemed that lately, there'd been too much death. Surely they were due some good news soon? He thought as he took a draw on his pipe.

He finally managed to doze for a couple of hours in the chair by the fire. He woke in the early hours of the morning stiff from sleeping sitting up. He stood up and stretched before going in to check on his wife.

Martha was still sleeping and Fred didn't want to disturb her after her ordeal, so quietly cut a chunk of cheese and grab a slab of bread before leaving for work. As promised, he called upon the doctor on the way to work.

The day went slowly. He was desperate to check on his wife, but knew that he had to be patient if he were to do his job properly. That evening he hurried home and found Martha stirring a pot of broth.

"Shouldn't you be in bed?" He asked.

Martha looked round at him, and it was obvious that she'd been crying. Fred wanted to go to her, but there was something on her face that stopped him. He looked at her expectantly.

"Fred, I know how much you want children and as I said yesterday, I'm too old to try again. I want you to go and find somebody who can give you a family."

Fred looked at her and took a step back.

"We've been through this. I don't want anybody else. I want you and if that means we don't have children then so be it. Now, let's put an end to this nonsense." he said sternly.

Martha turned abruptly back to the broth, tears threatening to cascade down her pale cheeks. She wasn't sure whether they were in relief that Fred didn't want to leave her, or sorrow for her husband who'd married a barren woman. *How can he love me when I can't even give him what he most desires?* She thought despondently.

CHAPTER THIRTEEN

Martha couldn't help the feeling that Fred would be better off without her. *If he were with someone else he could have children*, was the thought that niggled at her incessantly, whenever she was alone.

Maybe I could let him have a child with another woman, she thought, before shaking her head vigorously. She knew she couldn't stand by and watch as he fathered children with someone else.

She thought about leaving him, but just the thought of it filled her with dread. *I'm just not strong enough,* she thought, *and anyway, where would I go? My parents wouldn't understand why I'd do such a thing.*

Maybe our only choice is a baby farm? But how would we know if the procurer was a good sort? The Government is already talking of regulating foster carers, because of how badly the children are treated and I don't think I could bear to see the little mites who end up in that sort of place.

Fred could see how unhappy she was and didn't know what to do to get her understand that she was the most important thing in his life.

As he sat there, his thoughts turned to his job, which he loved, though he still felt a huge weight on his shoulders from not being able to save Thomas from his early demise.

Deep in thought he looked up startled, as Martha placed her hand on his shoulder and looked tenderly down at him.

"Are you okay?" She asked.

"I was just thinking about that poor boy. I should have done more to stop it."

"It wasn't your fault."

"I should have told the men to refuse to work. To down tools. Frank would have had to do something then."

"But haven't you always told me that Frank's a good man? It was an accident, and if you hadn't been there, somebody else would have made the same decision as you."

Fred looked up at his wife. He closed his eyes and scratched his head.

"But that doesn't make it right though, does it?" He asked

She nodded and said, "No, I suppose not."

"I need to speak with Frank again. He doesn't believe that we should stop the machines to clean underneath them. He tells me that productivity is too important to stop the machines, but maybe now that he's got another death on his hands, maybe things would be different." Fred said sadly.

He sat there in his own thoughts for a moment longer. Martha turned back to the kitchen and continued with her ironing. *I'll speak with him today*, he decided as he stood up.

He walked over to his wife and gave her a quick peck on the cheek, before walking to the door, with a heavy feeling in his heart.

As he walked slowly up the hill towards the factory,

he wondered what he would do if Frank still refused to allow the children to wait for the machines to shut down before cleaning under them.

Would I really hand my notice in? He wondered. *What would we do for money? It's all well and good having strong principles, but they don't put bread on the table.*

Fred walked through the gates, nodding to the men as they walked in alongside him. They seemed to know he wasn't in the mood to talk and most gave him a wide berth, leaving him to wallow in his thoughts.

He turned into one of the corridors that led towards the stairs to the offices and noticed a slight shadow out of the corner of his eye. His brow furrowed as he thought back to other times, when he'd had a feeling that someone was lurking in the shadows.

The feeling didn't feel him with a sense of dread, but actually gave him some comfort, though he wasn't sure why. *I must investigate it at some point and find out what's going on, but first I need to get to see Frank and try to persuade him that he needs to take the welfare of his men more seriously,* he thought as he started up the stairs to the offices

Annie had woken late, after struggling to get to sleep

again and was scurrying towards the shop floor, when she saw Fred coming towards her. She scampered into a tight corner and held her breath, hoping he hadn't seen her.

She waited a full five minutes until she was sure that no one was out there looking for her. She poked her head around the corner of the column she'd hidden behind and then satisfied she was alone, she squeezed her thin body out into the open.

Her eyes darted around as she nervously looked to see if anyone was hiding, waiting to grab her round the shoulders, but no one did. She gave a sigh of relief as she continued, still cautiously towards the machines to start work.

She had decided she would do her utmost to stay away from under the machines, but she knew John wouldn't be able to help her, if she didn't do the tasks she was given.

As Fred climbed the stairs, his feet seemed to get heavier with every step he took towards Franks office. He was dreading the conversation, but knew he couldn't put it off any longer. *I won't be able to rest until something's been done to make the job safer*, he thought.

He took a deep breath and knocked purposefully on Frank's door.

"Yes" he heard a loud voice boom from within the office.

Fred pushed the door open and walked into the office. He strode over to the desk with a confidence he didn't feel and stood in front of Frank, standing as straight as he could.

"Good morning, Fred." Frank said.

"Good morning Sir."

"I suppose this is about the other day? That poor boy, terrible thing to have happened."

"Yes." said Fred, plonking himself on the seat opposite Frank before he'd been given a chance to be offered it.

Fred closed his eyes and thought for a moment, unsure how to start the conversation.

"Frank, I know you're a good man, but we can't go on like this. We need to do something to make sure we never get another death like that again."

"I know you're right." Frank said. "I should have listened to you last week when you came in."

Fred smiled. Maybe we can work something out, he thought optimistically.

Frank cleared his throat.

"I've been thinking about your plan to clean under the machines while they're not operating. How will that work exactly? Is there anyway we can speed up the start up operation, so the machines aren't sat around idle? And how will we makes sure the machines stay clean? If they start getting cotton caught up in them, they'll break down. There's so much to think about, Fred." The words spewed out of his mouth like a torrent he couldn't stop.

Fred looked at Frank and nodded emphatically. Pulling his shoulders back he smiled.

"Well, sir. I've been talking to the men and we think there may be a way of decreasing the startup time of the machines, and as for making sure the machines are properly maintained, well…"

They continued discussing and planning a solution which could improve health and safety without compromising productivity. After an hour with their heads together, they came out with what they thought could work.

"Are you sure the men will agree to it?" Frank asked.

"I'll pull them all together later and ask them. I think if I explain everything to them, they'll be happy to go along with the changes. If I can show them it will improve health and safety then I don't think they're going to have any problems with it. You never know sir, this might even increase productivity."

"Let's hope you're right." Said Frank smiling.

Fred stood up and shook Frank's hand before turning to leave. As he reached the door he looked over his shoulder at his boss.

"Thanks sir, I'm sure you won't regret it." He said gratefully.

"I'm sure I won't. Thank you Fred." Frank replied.

As Fred went downstairs to the shop floor he remembered the shadow he'd seen earlier. *As soon as our shift's over, I'm going to find out exactly what that was,* he told himself.

As he entered the machine room, he felt a lightness he hadn't felt in a long while. *Everything's going to work itself out, I just know it,* he thought as he smiled at everyone hard at work.

CHAPTER FOURTEEN

The rest of the day passed smoothly, and Fred didn't have many problems to worry about, apart from a couple of times when one of the machines threatened to go down. But the engineer took a quick look at it and managed to fix it before any big problems happened.

At the end of the shift he called everyone together and told them what he'd agreed with the mill owner.

"If the machines aren't working so long, then what does that mean for our wages?" Someone asked.

The murmurs got louder as everyone expressed their fears of job losses and pay cuts. Fred put his hands up to silence them. As the noise died down he continued.

"Look, we think we can get the machines set up

quicker, so there won't be any additional downtime so that won't affect your wages. We need to think about your welfare as well, we don't want no repeat of the incident the other day, now do we?"

A few of them shook their heads and Fred smiled looking them straight in the eyes.

"We're going to trial it from next week, and if you got any concerns, you just need to voice them during the trial and we'll see what happens. Is that okay?"

The workers nodded, whispering to each other about how they would be happy to try anything that made their lives safer.

"Go on then, off to see your families." He said, dismissing them for the day.

As they walked out a couple of the men stopped and turned to him.

"Fancy a pint Fred?"

Fred smiled, thinking he must be doing something right, if they still wanted to drink with him.

"No, you're all right. I got a few things I need to deal with first." He told them.

As he watched them leaving, he turned towards the machines. He was determined to find out what was lurking in the shadows. *I hope it ain't a rat*, he thought giggling at his nervousness. He knew it was too big to be an animal, but for the life of him couldn't think what it could be.

He started to follow the corridor down to the stairs which led to the offices. There were plenty of dark spaces there, that someone or something could hide. He wandered under the big pipes overhead and saw something from the corner of his eye. He tried to follow it, but it darted out of sight.

He followed his instincts and followed one of the pipes into a small engine room. Suddenly he saw a little girl in the shadows underneath the stairwell.

"Oy, you, What are you doing 'ere?" he shouted, as he strode towards her.

Annie felt trapped. She pulled herself into a little ball, with her arms around her knees, trying as if to make herself invisible. Her eyes darted around as she looked for some way of escaping.

Fred towered above her, his brown wavy hair falling in front of his face as he leant towards her. He looked at her sternly with his dark brown eyes and put his hands on his bent knees.

"I said, what are you doing 'ere?" He repeated, as he reached out and grabbed her by the shoulders in order to make sure he didn't lose her.

Annie cowered even further back. Fred could see that she was terrified and so, knelt down until he was nearly at face level.

"Who are you? And what are you doing here?" he asked more gently.

As Annie told him all about how she'd escaped from the workplace, Fred gasped.

"And then I ended up in the town and it was so busy. I nearly died." She said, as she told him about nearly falling into the road and being hit by the tram.

"But how did you get here?" He asked, still perplexed at how this little slip of a girl, could have managed to experience so much in such as short lifetime.

"I snuck in Sir. Then I met Thomas and I been 'elping clean out underneath them machines."

"And were you there when…" Fred's voice trailed off as he didn't know how to finish the sentence, though he hoped that for some reason she'd not seen the accident.

"Yes." She said, tears welling up as she remembered seeing Thomas lying prone on the shop floor.

"Oh." He said gently, knowing how he'd felt at the time and knowing it must have been a hundred times worse for this youngster.

"And what have you been doing for food?" He asked.

As they'd been talking, Fred had taken his arms off of Annie's shoulders. She looked furtively around for a chance to escape and as he asked her the question, she squirmed out of her hiding place and ran.

Fred gave chase, but his limp prevented him from moving as fast as her.

"Oy, come back. I'm not going to hurt you." He called after her.

He followed the direction she'd run in and searched for a bit longer, but she was nowhere to be seen. He decided to cut his losses and go home. He thought she'd probably left the mill and wondered if she might be gone for good.

CHAPTER FIFTEEN

"You're late." Said Martha. Fred always came home straight from work and she'd begun to worry that something had happened.

"I know, sorry love." He said as he planted a kiss on her cheek.

He sat down at the table and told Martha about the little girl he'd found hiding in the mill.

"She saw little Thomas's accident, and had no one to comfort her."

"Oh, the poor thing." Martha cried out instinctively.

"Where's she now?" She asked.

" I don't know. She ran off, first chance she's got. I searched, but I think she's left the building."

"So she's out on the streets alone, somewhere?" Martha's eyes widened as she realised that this little girl had no one to take care of her.

"What happened to her parents?" She asked.

"Seems like her mother died and her father, well he left her there, at the workhouse." Fred said, repeating what Annie had told him.

"How could somebody do that to a little girl? To their own daughter? She asked, shocked at the very thought.

"I don't know. She seems such a nice, kind but timid girl." Fred said sadly.

"You need to find her, bring her home."

Fred looked at Martha, raising his eyebrows at the fervour in her voice.

"Are you sure? We don't know much about her at all. I've only just met her, she could be a con artist, a thief, anything." Fred warned, not wanting his wife to let her emotions get too involved.

"You've said yourself, she seems a nice girl. She can't be living on the streets alone. She needs to have somebody to care about her. Go and find her."

Fred nodded slowly with pursed lips.

"Okay, but it'll have to wait until morning. I'll never find her now, not in the darkness of them alleyways. I'll go first thing, I promise." He told his wife.

Martha looked at him, wanting to argue but knowing he was right. If the little girl was too scared to come back, then Fred would never find her now it was dark.

Martha tossed and turned all night. Every time she dozed off, she would dream about the little girl lost in the darkness, being chased by all sorts of predators.

Finally as day broke she decided to get up and get the fire in the stove going. She made herself a cup of tea and prepared Fred's breakfast *so he can get off first thing, like he promised,* she thought.

Fred woke blurry eyed. He'd not slept well either. The little girl's fate also weighing heavily on his mind. He pulled on his clothes and limped over to the table. His leg always gave him more gip first thing, though he knew by lunchtime, he'd hardly notice it.

He grabbed the breakfast that Martha had prepared and then sat back and drank his tea. Martha watched him with her hands on her hips and finally he stood up and laughed.

"I'm going... no need to look at me like that."

Lowering her head, Martha blushed.

"I'm sorry, love. It's just that I'm worried about that little girl."

"I know, me too." Fred said, patting her on the arm.

He flung his coat over his shoulders and said, "I'll be back as soon as possible."

He gave Martha a quick peck on the cheek and moved towards the door.

"Do you want to take a piece of bread and jam, just in case she's hungry?" Asked Martha.

"It'll be all right. I'll bring her straight here, ten minutes more won't hurt. That's if I find her, mind." He warned his wife.

I hope she isn't getting her hopes up too much, he thought as he walked towards the market. *There's so many street urchins. Who's going to remember just one?* As he reached the square he looked around, not knowing where to start.

Being Saturday it was busier than normal. Less people worked on the weekend and they would go to WesleyField Square and get a few bits in ready for their Sunday lunch. The flies swarmed around the meat stall and Fred could hear the sounds of the grocer advertising his wares. A dog ran past him and nearly knocked him over as it suddenly turned to chase a cat. A nearby costermonger was selling whelks and oysters from a large basket he held over his arm.

He wandered the streets, talking to the street traders and shop owners, asking them if they'd seen a little girl, who fitted Annie's description.

Everybody just shook their heads and shrugged. There were so many orphans that roamed the streets, begging and trying to steal, that the traders became quite blind to them all.

"She might 'av been taken by the police. They do their best to round them up and if she ain't used to being out 'ere, then she'd not know where to hide." One of them told her, taking pity on this man's foolhardy mission.

Fred had nodded. He knew it to be true, however much him and Martha hated the thought. As lunchtime came closer he decided he was wasting his time and turned to go back home.

As he did so, he saw a costermonger, standing at the end of an alley, trying to catch shoppers on their way out of the market.

He walked over and smiled.

"Good morning. I'm looking for a little girl. Yey high." He said, putting his hand to about the height he thought she might be.

"She's got dark auburn hair in ringlets, big brown eyes with these unusually long eyelashes. Don't suppose you've seen 'er?

The costermonger scratched his chin for a moment, looking upwards in thought.

"I think I saw 'er earlier today." He said finally, after Fred had decided he had forgotten about him.

"She were hanging round the baker's over there, but he told 'er to scoot."

Fred's face lit up. *Maybe I will find her,* he thought.

"Do you know what direction she went in?" He asked hopefully.

The costermonger thought again for a minute. Fred stood trying not to tap his foot to obviously.

"That way, I think... no, I'm sure of It." He said, rubbing his chin, before pointing the opposite way to that Fred had been walking.

"Thanks." Said Fred as he turned away. *Shall I carry*

on home, or should I give it just one more shot, he thought to himself.

CHAPTER SIXTEEN

Fred knew that Martha would never forgive him if he didn't follow the lead he'd been given, so although his feet were sore and his knee was aching he turned in the direction he'd been pointed to.

As he passed the end of one of the alleyways, something caught his eye. He noticed something small huddled in the shadows. He crept towards the bundle. He was certain that it was the girl and didn't want to do anything to startle her.

As he reached her, she looked up, eyes bulging as she realised they were coming for her. She stood up quickly and went to run, but Fred managed to grab her shoulder and stopped her in her tracks. As she looked up into his face she recognised him from the mill and looked at him bewildered. She'd assumed it was a policemen, ready to take her back to the workhouse. She was petrified that she'd be sent back there and be beaten for running away.

"Please, sir, don't take me to the police."

Fred knelt down and placed his hand over hers.

"I've not come to take you to the police. I've come to take you home."

Annie felt faint with exhaustion and confusion.

"What do you mean take me home?" She asked in a high pitched voice. "I ain't got no home."

"My wife is worried about you. She wanted me to come and find you and bring you home with me. Come on. We'll get you something to eat when we get there."

He took Annie by the hand and led her back to the house. Annie followed curiously, not knowing whether to drag her heels. *Who is this man and what does he want with me?* She thought taking another sidelong glance at Fred. Fred was determined to get her back to Martha, so made sure he didn't loosen his grip on the little girl.

He pushed open the door and called out to Martha, who rushed over.

"Hello." She said as she knelt down in front of Annie, putting her hands on Annie's shoulders.

"Hello." Replied Annie timidly.

"I'm Martha and this is Fred." Martha told her, pointing to her husband.

Annie eyes darted between the two of them, not knowing where to look.

"What's your name?" Martha asked.

"An..n..ie…" She stammered.

"Well, Annie, come along and I'll get you some food."

Martha put her arm around Annie's shoulder and led her to the kitchen table, where she sat her down. She turned to the side and cut a thick slice of bread before spreading it thickly with jam. She handed it to the little girl who looked at her silently before grabbing it out of her hand.

As Annie scoffed it down hungrily, Martha felt her heart fill with joy. *She needs a bit of a scrub*, she thought, *but she's just precious*.

She smiled at Annie

"You know Annie, you remind me of my niece, Daisy. She's a little younger than you, I think, but about the same size."

Annie looked at her still bewildered at what was happening. She didn't have any family and wasn't sure what a niece was. She nodded cautiously though, as she didn't want this couple to think she was rude.

Martha started to ask her questions, and Annie did her best to answer them. Annie could feel her eyelids growing heavy and as much as she tried to force them to stay open she started to doze. Her head jerked back as she started to lean forward and Martha sighed softly.

"Okay, maybe I'll leave the questions to later. First, I think we need to get some of that grime off of you. Then you might like a nap. Fred you make yourself scarce for a time, and Annie, come here, we'll take off those dirty clothes you're wearing and clean you up. Maybe put a brush through your hair." She said standing up and turning her head sharply to Fred.

Annie looked nervously as Fred took his leave and Martha helped pull her dress over her head. With some water from the kettle, Martha took a soft cloth and scrubbed Annie all over.

After she stood back and looked at Annie.

"Why, what a pretty little thing you are. I think I've

got one of Daisy's dresses somewhere."

She looked around and picked up a dress that her sister had left there for when Daisy stayed over.

"Here. Let's put it on you. Get rid of that dirty old thing you've been wearing."

She pulled the dress over Annie's head and smoothed it down before smiling at the girl stood before her.

Annie looked down at herself in wonderment. She'd never felt so clean or smelled so nice. She touched the lace that edged the sleeves with her long fingers. Then reached up and felt around her neck. Her eyes sparkled as she felt joy bubble inside her stomach. She twirled around in delight and Martha laughed as she watched her.

As Annie realised she was being watched, she stopped in embarrassment.

"It's okay. You carry on." Said Martha happily.

"It's so nice to see a child in the house."

Annie smiled shyly and yawned.

"Well, we need to find you somewhere to sleep." Said Martha and looked around as Fred came back in with some small pieces of wood for the fire. She looked over at her husband and smiled warmly at him.

"Annie, you can stay here tonight. And if you like it, you can live with us forever. That'd be all right, wouldn't it Fred?"

"Of course it would." Replied Fred.

"If that's what Annie would like."

Annie looked at the couple. She didn't really know what was going on, but she'd understood that they were offering her a home. She grinned at them both, as Martha took her hand and lay her down on a small pile of blankets that Fred put down by the fire.

"You can sleep here for tonight and if you want to stay, we can make you up a more permanent bed upstairs for tomorrow." Fred told Annie.

As Annie drifted off, exhausted from the last few days, she snuggled deeper into the blankets, feeling more comfortable than she could ever remember being.

CHAPTER SEVENTEEN

"No. Please, don't. I'll be good, I promise." Annie called out, as she tossed and turned, in her sleep.

Martha woke with a start and realised that Annie was having a nightmare. She jumped out of bed and ran over to Annie. She knelt down beside her and put her hand on Annie's arm.

"It's okay, my sweet, Annie." She said gently. "No one's going to hurt you here, You're safe now."

Annie opened her eyes suddenly, a thin layer of perspiration covering her young body. She looked up at Martha, slowly realising where she was.

"I'm sorry." She said timidly.

"You've got nothing to be sorry about." Martha chided her. "Now, get back to sleep. I'll stay with you, for a while."

Annie nodded and slid back under the covers and was soon sleeping again.

Martha waited a little while longer, then crept back to her bed and slid in next to Fred, trying not to wake him.

"Is she okay?" Fred whispered, as Martha pulled the blanket over her.

"She's sleeping now." Martha whispered back.

The next morning, as Annie was getting dressed, Martha talked to Fred about Annie's nightmares.

"We need to do something about them." She said. "I can't bear the thought of what she must have gone through at that place."

Fred patted her arm.

"Don't distress yourself. I'm in agreement. I think I'm going to go to the authorities and make a complaint. See what they say about it all."

"You really think they'll do anything?" Martha asked.

Fred shrugged.

"We can but try." He said, matter of factly.

"When do you think you'll go?" Martha pressed.

"As soon as I can. I'll ask Frank if I can have an hour off, go into work a bit late. He don't like bullies, so he don't. I'm sure he'll oblige."

Martha nodded happily, grateful that her husband was taking it so seriously.

"But let's not tell Annie anything about it. I don't want her worrying that something might happen to her." She said.

"I agree." Said Fred, "Now, what are your plans for today?" He asked, putting an end to their whispering as he noticed Annie coming closer.

Martha smiled and looked over at Annie.

"Well, my sister's coming round with Daisy. I'm going to introduce her to Annie, so that she'll have a friend at school."

Fred raised his eyebrows. He supposed he'd known that Annie would need to go to school, but hadn't really thought about the practicalities of how to go about it.

"Yes, of course, school." He said grinning at Annie. "You did school at the workhouse, did you?" He asked her, suddenly realising that he knew very little about what happened in a workhouse. He'd heard stories obviously, but didn't really know what Annie had gone through. *Maybe I should spend some time finding out about them,* he thought as he straightened his cravat.

Annie nodded, not quite meeting his gaze. She'd quite liked learning, but was nervous about going to a new school, where she wouldn't know anyone.

"You've already missed a couple of months of education, and we don't want the authorities to find any reason to tell us that you can't stay now, do we?" Fred asked her gently.

Annie shook her head, looking down at her feet.

Fred knelt in front of her. He had a question that he couldn't put off any longer.

"And Annie, there's one more thing to discuss."

Annie looked at him, with wide eyes.

"I need to know who was helping you at the factory. Someone must have been giving you food and helping you out. Whomever it were, they'll be worried about you. Not knowing where you are. Can you see that?"

Annie nodded and looked back down at the floor.

"I promised." She whispered.

Fred took her hands in his and smiled softly at the little girl in front on him.

"I promise he won't get into trouble, but I need to let him know you're safe. He may have done wrong in some people's eyes, but I'm so glad he did what he did. It's not like he's going to come forward on his own, do you understand?"

Annie was silent for a moment, and then whispered, "His name was John. He was very kind. Please don't tell him off."

Fred knew instinctively which of the John's it was that would have gone out of his way to help her.

"Could you describe him to me?" Fred asked, wanting to check, before talking to the wrong man and perhaps dropping her guardian angel in it.

"He were very tall, with dark hair and big hands." Annie said.

"Did he have a moustache that went up on the ends?" Asked Fred.

Annie smiled and nodded enthusiastically . "Yes, he used to twirl it when he was talking to me and Thomas."

Fred smiled. He knew exactly who she was talking about. He decided he would try to talk to him on the quiet as early as possible. It had been a few days since Annie had been at the factory and John was probably worried about her disappearance.

"Anyway, I'd better go, got work to do and mouths to feed." He said, winking at Annie as he stood up and grabbed his coat off the hook on the back of the door.

Annie chewed her lip as she watched him leave. Going over to where Martha was busy clearing away the breakfast things she took a deep breath, not knowing if she was going to like the answer to her question.

"Can you afford to feed me?" She asked.

Martha laughed.

"Of course we can."

"But Fred said…" Annie continued.

"I heard. He was just making a joke." Martha said shrugging it off.

"Now, why don't you help me tidy up this kitchen, ready for my sister and niece to come visit."

Annie happily wiped the cups and plates dry and put them away where Martha told her to.

For lunch they had a thin piece of bread and jam and soon after, there was a knock at the door.

"That'll be our Flora." Martha said, wiping her hands on her apron.

"Come in." She called out.

CHAPTER EIGHTEEN

Annie stood where she was, frozen to the spot.

"Come on Annie. Come and say hello." Martha said reaching out her hand to the girl.

Annie tucked her hair behind her ear and walked over hesitantly. She held out her hand to the woman stood next to Martha and looked up at her through her eyelashes. Flora smiled at Annie and bent down so she was on the same level as her.

"Why aren't you a pretty little thing." She said, touching Annie gently on her cheek. "My sister sent me a letter telling me all about you. Daisy here has been desperate to meet her new cousin."

Annie looked around at Daisy who was stood there

smiling and carrying two of her dolls. Daisy walked over and held one of them out to Annie.

"This one is for you." She said.

Annie stared at her bewilderedly.

"For me?" She asked, not believing it could be so.

"Yes. I have some more at home. My mother thought it would be nice to share one with you, now you are part of our family."

Annie took the doll and smiled shyly at Daisy, before casting her eyes on her present. She'd had a doll when her mother had been alive, but it hadn't been in the bundle that her father had given to her when he had left her at the workhouse.

"Thank you Daisy. That's so kind of you." Said Martha, clasping her hand to her chest.

"Now, why don't you two go over there and play?"

The two girls sat down on the rug and after a little awkwardness, began to play with the dolls and soon became friends. Martha and Flora watched as the two little girls giggled.

"She seems such a nice girl." Flora said. "But what do you really know about her?" She asked, concerned about what her sister might be getting herself into.

Martha shrugged, tilting her head up.

"Nothing really. Fred was worried at first, that she might run off with our stuff, but she's settled in find. She's a lovely little thing, very helpful and very polite."

Flora nodded, twisting the ring on her finger, not knowing what to say.

"But Flora, you should see the poor mite. If you turn towards her a bit quickly, she cowers, and she has the most awful nightmares. We think she was beaten at the workhouse." She lowered her voice conspiratorially.

"In fact Fred is going to speak to the authorities. Ask them to investigate." She told her sister.

"Are you sure you want to get involved in that sort of thing?" Flora asked, lowering her head towards Martha.

Martha knew her sister was well intentioned, but couldn't believe that she would rather turn a blind eye than do something to stop such abuse.

"Of course. I couldn't bear the thought of those children being beaten. What if it were Daisy?" She asked pointedly.

Flora closed her eyes, and shuddered at the very idea.

"I know you're right. I just worry about you." She

replied.

"I know, but I'm sure people will understand why we're doing it, and if they don't, they don't." Martha said more bravely than she was feeling.

Flora looked at her sister. *I hope I'd be able to do what they're doing, if it came to it,* she thought as her heart swelled with a sense of pride.

They watched the two children playing for a little while longer. Annie was teaching Daisy how to play jacks with some stones she'd picked up from outside. It was a game that Sarah had taught her not long after they'd become friends, and Annie sighed deeply as she remembered their times together.

Flora finished her second cup of tea and then started gathering her belongings. She stood up and went over and put her hand on Daisy's shoulder.

"Come on, young lady. Time to go." She said with a smile. "You'll see Annie again tomorrow at school."

Daisy stood up, picking up her doll as she did so.

"Bye Annie. See you tomorrow." She said politely.

Then she walked over to Martha and wrapped her arms around her.

"Bye Aunt Martha, I'm so happy that you've got your

own little girl now."

Martha couldn't help the tears that welled up in her eyes.

"Daisy is so wise for her years." She mouthed to her sister.

Flora smiled and blushed. Her daughter was turning into a kind and thoughtful young girl and she felt a warmth flood her body as her sister recognised it out loud. She nodded proudly.

"Nice to meet you Annie." She said turning to the new arrival.

"Good bye." Annie hesitated, not sure what to call Martha's sister.

Flora smiled at her uncertainty. "You'd better call me Aunt Flora." She told Annie.

Annie took a deep breath and gulped before saying. "Good bye Daisy, good bye Aunt Flora."

Martha smiled at Annie. She'd done her proud and she was glad that she'd got on with Daisy. She was just hoping that it would be the same tomorrow when she had a classroom full of new children to meet. She had gasped, shocked at the very idea, when Annie had asked if the teachers would beat her, telling her that no one would ever beat her again. With a knot in her stomach, she thought, *I hope nothing happens that makes me have to break that promise.*

CHAPTER NINETEEN

Much to Martha's delight, Annie skipped out of school the next day, laughing with one of the other children. Walking home, she was full of chatter about how much fun she'd had, how nice the children were and was especially enchanted with her teacher.

"The teacher at the workhouse was quite kind, but she was scared of Matron. Matron would get really cross with her if she caught her being nice to us." Annie explained to Martha.

Martha gave her a wry smile and said, "That woman can't hurt you now."

Annie nodded but Martha could still see the doubt in her eyes. Annie continued to tell Martha all about her day, quickly forgetting the sick feeling that filled her stomach every time she thought about her old life.

Martha listened to Annie prattling on and smiled. *I hope she'll always be that carefree, she deserves it, after what she's been through,* she thought as she drifted off to her childhood.

They hadn't had much, but her mother and father had always tried to make sure that they were well dressed and had plenty of food on the table at meal times. *I wish they were still around to meet Annie*, she thought wistfully.

Suddenly Martha felt a tug on the sleeve of her coat. She looked down at Anne who was looking at her worriedly.

"What is it? Is everything okay?" She asked, looking around to see what it might be.

"I asked you a question, but I don't think you heard." Annie replied timidly.

Martha smiled and apologised.

"I was thinking back to when I was your age." She said.

Annie looked at her and with a sharp intake of breath said, "That was a long time ago."

Martha couldn't help the big belly laugh that erupted out of her mouth. *Out of the mouths of babes*, she thought smirking.

"It was indeed." She replied. "Now what were you asking me?" She said, trying to get the conversation back on track.

"Well, I wanted to know if you could have more than one friend?" Annie asked. "Daisy is my best friend, but I also like Mary, is that all right."

Martha bent so she could look directly into Annie's eyes.

"You can have as many friends as you like. If they're good friends, they will be happy that you have lots of friends."

Annie nodded happily and then started skipping down the street in front of Martha. Martha quickened her step. She was nervous that Annie would get lost, even though Annie looked back every minute or so, to make sure Martha was still in sight.

Once they got home, Annie put on her apron and rolled up her sleeves. She called Annie to her and showed her how to start preparing the vegetables for their evening meal together.

Annie settled in well at school and soon had lots of new friends. Daisy remained her closest friend and sometimes it was as though they were sisters, rather than cousins.

Flora would occasionally walk home from school with Martha and have a cup of tea, while the two children sat and played together.

With her elbow on the kitchen table watching the children chattering incessantly Flora noticed Martha watching her. Blushing slightly, Flora said quickly, "What do you think they're talking about?"

Martha laughed. I've got no idea." She replied, turning to look at the two young girls sitting on the rug.

"If I remember rightly, no good probably." Flora said, winking at her sister.

They both laughed at the memories of when they were young.

Like Martha and Flora, the two girls had got into a couple of scrapes, but nothing serious. If they got scolded for something they would hastily apologise and promise not to do it again.

The neighbours adored Annie and always smiled and waved at her when she skipped past their doorstep.

Annie would make sure she waved at everyone as she skipped past them and would occasionally go and sit with the elderly woman next door who didn't have any family of her own.

One morning, not long after Fred had left for work, Martha and Annie were getting ready for school. Annie noticed Martha rubbing her stomach.

"Are you all right?" She asked.

Martha smiled. "Yes, just a little uncomfortable. Now come on, let's get ready for school, before you're late. And just to let you into a little secret, me and Fred have a surprise to tell you this evening."

Annie looked at her apprehensively. She wasn't sure she liked surprises. She didn't want to wait until that evening but was too scared to say anything. She quickly got her things together and rushed out the door in front of Martha who slowly stood up and followed her.

That evening when Fred came in from work, Martha beckoned him over to the stove.

"We're going to have to tell her today. She's noticed something is amiss and I don't want to worry her."

Fred nodded uncertainly.

"Are you sure?" He asked. "What will we tell her?"

"The truth." Martha replied arching her eyebrows at him.

"When?" He whispered.

"Now." Martha whispered back, feeling a nervous giggle building inside her.

"Okay, just let me get my coat off." He said, wandering back to the door to hang his coat off and take off his shoes.

"Annie." Martha called over to the little girl who was playing with her doll on the rug.

Annie stood up and came over.

"Yes?" She asked.

"Remember this morning I said we had a surprise to tell you?"

Annie nodded.

"Well sit down and we'll tell you our secret."

Annie sat at the table wringing her hands in her lap, unable to keep still.

"It's nothing to worry about." Martha told her, noticing how anxious she looked. She took her hands and placed them on the table in front of Annie.

"Me and Fred are having a baby."

Annie lifted her head sharply and looked first at Martha and then at Fred. She had no idea where babies came from and didn't really understand what it all meant.

Noticing her confusion, Martha stood up and walked around the table to where Annie was sitting. She took Annie's hand and placed it on her stomach.

"In here is either a little boy or girl, and in about four months we'll have a new baby."

Annie looked at her not knowing what to say.

Martha was disappointed. When she'd realised she'd not had her monthlies for a few months, she had done the calculations.

Neither she or Fred had been able to hide their excitement when those calculations had revealed she was over the three months mark. None of her previous pregnancies had gotten that far and they felt that this child was finally meant to be.

Annie looked at them for a little longer and then in a quiet voice asked if she might leave the table. Fred looked at Martha and raised his eyebrows. Martha pouted and shrugged her shoulders.

Later that evening, once Annie had gone to bed, Fred

said in a low voice, "What was that all about? I thought she'd be excited about having a baby brother or sister."

Martha shrugged.

"I don't know. I suppose, she's still learning how to be a part of this family and this is another change that she has to deal with. She's already had so much go on in her short life, that maybe she's not sure how to react to good news." She said, trying to persuade herself as much as her husband.

Fred screwed up his nose in thought.

"She'll come around, I'm sure of it." He said finally. He tried to sound confident, but he had a funny feeling that life was about to become even more complicated.

CHAPTER TWENTY

Annie woke up the next day, with an anxious feeling in the pit of her stomach. The news she'd been told yesterday had unsettled her more than she know how to explain, even to herself.

The thoughts whirled around her head like a tornado, *what if they don't want me, why do they need me if they have their own child, what if they can't afford to keep me and the baby, what if they can't cope with more than one child, what if they leave me at the workhouse, like my father did.* She couldn't help herself and the more the thoughts swirled, the bigger the knot in her stomach became.

She thought about confiding in Daisy, but realised she might feel disloyal to her aunt, if she was asked not

not to say anything. *What if my worries come true? What if they haven't thought about it yet, if I say anything they might realise I'm right.*

She decided that she needed to do something before they came to the same conclusions she had. *I can't go back to the workhouse, I just can't. Not now,* she told herself.

She began to make a plan. *It's getting colder, so I'll need warm clothes, and some food, at least until I can find a job,* she thought. She had learnt from her disappearance from the workhouse and knew she had to be more organised this time around, if she wasn't going to fall into the same traps.

I'll start keeping a little bit of my food back, hide it somewhere, and when I've got enough. I'll go. I just hope they didn't send me back before that happens. While I'm getting everything together I'll start looking for somewhere I can stay, now I know the streets better.

As she continued to plan everything in her head, she could feel a heaviness in her body. *I'll miss them so much. I wish I didn't have to go,* she thought.

She dragged her heels on the way to school. She was worried that Daisy would notice that something was amiss and hated the thought of hiding anything from her.

After school, Daisy asked if Annie wanted to play, but Annie shook her head and told her she was too tired. Daisy tried to get her to change her mind, but Annie was too distressed to take any notice.

Martha watched Annie anxiously as she seemed to have the weight of the world on her young shoulders.

"Are you okay?" She asked.

With great difficultly Annie met her gaze and nodded. She was worried if she opened her mouth that all the words would come tumbling out.

"You'd tell me if you weren't?" Asks Martha, trying to get through to the little girl.

Annie nodded again, before turning towards the table where her doll was sat.

She picked up her doll and sat down on the rug, hugging it tightly to her. *I'll need to remember to take you,* she whispered into its paper mache head.

Martha knew that Annie was sad, but didn't know what to say to make everything better. She hoped she was just feeling a little unsettled about the new baby. *Maybe in a few days Annie will see that the baby wouldn't change the way we feel about her,* she thought chewing the inside of her bottom lip.

When Fred came in he asked quietly, "How is she today?"

"Quiet. I don't know what to do." Martha admitted.

"We can't do anything more than we're doing. I don't think. We just have to show her that she is important to us. She'll come around, you mark my words." Fred said confidently.

"I hope you're right." Said Martha as she started to busy herself getting the evening meal on the table.

Annie sat and slowly ate her meal, watching the two adults while she did so, waiting for an opportune time to stuff a slice of bread into her pocket. She felt bad for doing it. She couldn't help feel as though she was stealing from them, but she hoped they'd forgive her, when the time came for her to disappear.

As soon as she'd finished supper she said, "I'm tired. Can I go to bed now?"

Fred and Martha exchanged concerned looks, but nodded.

"Maybe you're coming down with something?" Martha suggested as she walked up the stairs with Annie to help her get ready for bed and to tuck her in.

Annie nodded, but knew that wasn't why she was feeling so low.

As she lay down, Martha placed her cool hand on Annie's forehead.

"You don't feel like you've got a temperature." She said. "Maybe you just need a good nights sleep."

Annie nodded, then closed her eyes, waiting for Martha to leave.

Martha watched her for a minute, then gave a deep sigh, before turning and leaving the room.

As soon as Martha left the room, Annie got out of bed and snuck across the room to put the piece of bread in the drawer. It was little squashed, so she pressed it down flat before hiding it underneath her petticoats. She did the same thing the next evening and put a small apple in there with the bread. It had become dry overnight, but would be better than nothing when the time came.

Annie was at school and Martha had just finished the ironing. She sat down for a moment and closed her eyes. *Oh, if I sat here for too long, I'd fall asleep*, she thought as she put her hands on her knees and pushed herself upright.

Being with child, she found herself getting more fatigued and needing longer to finish her chores. She neatly folded the petticoats and dresses she'd ironed and then plodded up the stairs to the bedroom. She put the clothes on the bed, while she pulled open the drawer.

As she was placing the clothes on top of the pile, she noticed the apple peaking out. Frowning, she pulled back the clothes and saw the apple and two pieces of bread. She took a deep breath and then plodded over to the bed and sank down heavily.

What's that doing there? She thought. *Why on earth would Annie be hoarding food? I'll have to sit her down later and find out.*

For the rest of the day Martha's thoughts kept returning to the food she'd found. Pacing up and down the kitchen she searched for any answers as to why Annie might be hiding food. As much as she tired, she couldn't come up with an answer that sat right with her.

I wish Fred were here right now. Should I go to the factory and see if I can talk to him? She thought.

She decided that it wouldn't be wise to go to the factory. There was nothing Fred could do, even if she did manage to find him. He'd just worry, the same as her.

And they couldn't afford for him to lose his job. *No, I'll have to wait until Annie gets back from school and confront her. See what we've done to upset her.* She decided

By the time Martha collected Annie from school, she felt sick to her stomach. She grabbed Annie by the hand, desperate to get her home to discuss the food she'd found. Annie scampered behind, her short legs struggling to keep up.

She could sense something was wrong and was frighted that her fears had been realised. *What if she asks me to leave this evening? I don't' have enough food and I really don't want to leave. Why can't they let me stay, I'll be good, I won't get in the way,* she thought.

As soon as they removed their coats, Martha took Annie by the hand and led her over to the table.

"Annie, is everything okay?" she asked

Annie looked at her with teary eyes.

"Yes." She whispered, wringing her hands in front of her..

"Are you sure we haven't done anything to upset you?" Asked Martha.

Annie shook her head, but couldn't meet Martha's

gaze.

"It's just I found this in your drawer."

Martha leaned over to the shelf and took the food that she'd placed there.

"Oh." Said Annie, realising what it meant.

"Why did you hide the food?" Martha asked gently.

"I don't know." She replied, not wanting to acknowledge all her thoughts and feelings.

"Please tell me Annie. I can't help you, if I don't know what's wrong."

Annie sat there staring across from Martha, not knowing how to tell her that she was feeling lost and scared. That she was worried about being left again.

Martha could tell that she had a lot on her mind, but felt at a loss, not knowing how to cajole the answers out of the reticent little girl sat in front of her. *I hope Fred can help when he gets home,* she thought, deciding not to push Annie to hard for answers.

"All right. Well, go and play and maybe we can discuss this later?" Martha said finally.

Annie pushed her chair back and not raising her eyes to Martha slowly moved away, grabbing her doll and pulling it to her tightly, as if it was going to be taken away from her.

When Fred got home, Martha told him all about the food and the conversation she'd tried to have with Annie.

"Why won't she talk to us?" She asked. "Do you think she's unhappy with something?"

Fred put his arms around his wife, pulling her to him.

"I hope not." He said finally. "Maybe she doesn't like babies?"

"I don't think it's that." Martha said. "She loves her doll and I know that's not the same thing, but…" her voice trailed off as she realised she wasn't sure how she could explain it, she just knew she was right about it.

"Maybe she's worried about the baby taking her place?" He suggested.

Martha gasped. "Why didn't I think of that?"

She pinched the ridge of her nose hard, trying got think back to whether they'd said anything to make her think that. She couldn't recall anything, but knew in her gut that it was the answer. She looked into her husband's eyes.

"I think you've hit the nail on the head. Maybe we

just need to convince her that she's part of the family. Shall we say something at supper?" She asked.

Fred nodded, hoping that his wife would take the lead. He wasn't good with words, or discussing emotions and was already feeling drained from the conversation he'd had with John earlier that day.

As Martha started getting the table ready for their evening meal, Fred thought back to his exchange with John. At first he'd denied any knowledge of the little girl, but when he realised that Fred was thanking him, rather than reprimanding him, John had been more forthcoming.

"I know I shouldn't have done it, but she was such a tiny slip of a girl, like a little mouse in the shadows, I felt sorry for her, the poor thing, and she did work while she were here, I saw to that."

"And you gave her food?"

"Yes, well, someone had to. She wouldn't have survived on her own."

"Why didn't you take her in?" Asked Fred, thinking he knew the answer, but wanting to check.

"I got enough of me own at home. I couldn't really afford what I gave her. If I'd taken her 'ome, me wife would have left me." John said, winking.

Fred laughed, even though he knew John was only half joking. Wages weren't bad at the factory, but they didn't afford big families. With seven children at home, Fred knew that John would have sorely missed any food he gave up for little Annie.

"Well I appreciate it." He told the kind man in front of him. "She's with us now, and hopefully she'll want to stay with us for a very long time."

Now he thought back to those words, he wondered if he might have been a bit hasty. He wasn't a superstitious man, but he hoped he hadn't tempted fate by speaking too soon.

CHAPTER TWENTY ONE

As soon as supper was ready Fred called Annie over to the table. She walked over looking extremely subdued.

"Did you have a nice day at school?" He asked, trying to keep things as normal as possible.

With downcast eyes, Annie nodded as she picked up her spoon to eat the broth placed in front of her.

Martha sat down and started eating, trying to find the right words.

"You know, Annie. When this baby comes. I'm going to need you to be a big sister and help me look after him or her."

Annie's eyes widened and she put down her spoon.

"You're not sending me back to the workhouse?" She spluttered.

"What? Why would we have done that?" Martha exclaimed. She'd known that Annie was worried, but hadn't realised how deep her fears had been.

She put her hands over the table and placed them over Annies.

"You're not going anywhere. Not if you don't want to."

"But, if you've got your own child, why would you want…" Annie's voice trailed off. She didn't want to finish the sentence, as if it would make it true.

Martha gasped and stood up and took the few steps it took to reach the other side. Putting her arms around the back of Annie, she pulled her towards her chest.

"Annie, is that why you've been so upset these past few days?"

Annie kept her head down, but looked up through her eyelashes at Martha and gave a hesitant nod.

Martha sighed heavily.

" You are our very own child. I may not have had you here," she said, pointing to her stomach, "but we both love you as our daughter, don't we Fred?" She asked

asked looking over at him.

Fred cleared his throat. "You bet we do." He said gruffly.

"Even if we didn't there's no way that we would send you back to that place. In fact, Fred has been to the authorities and told them all about how you were treated there. They've promised to investigate, haven't they Fred." Martha continued, trying desperately to find a way of proving their love to Annie.

Annie's jaw dropped. "Do you really mean it? I can stay?" She asked hopefully.

"Of course," said Martha comfortingly, "would I lie to you?"

Annie breathed a deep sigh of relief. She shook her head, as if in response to the question, but also in disbelief.

"So does that mean that you won't be sneaking any more bread underneath your pillow"? Fred joked.

Annie looked at him and blushed a deep red. She smiled shyly, and shook her head, wishing she'd said something earlier and saved herself the worry.

"Good, that's settled then. You're staying and you can help Martha when the baby comes." He said matter of factly.

Annie smiled and felt a deep sense of relief flood her body. While Martha released her grip of Annie and went back to her seat, Fred continued.

"And I think it's high time that you started calling us mother and father, or ma and pa, if you'd prefer?"

Martha looked lovingly at her husband. *He's a good man and a good husband,* she thought, as she nodded her agreement.

Annie smile widened as she realised that she was finally home.

CHAPTER TWENTY TWO

Once Anne realised that Fred and Martha weren't sending her anywhere, she got very excited about the baby that was only a few months off from coming.

"And can I help feed her?" She asked Martha excitedly.

"What if it's a boy?" Martha responded.

Annie stopped and put her fingers to her lips. Martha could almost see the cogs whirring in the young girls brain. She smiled as she waited for the answer.

"I think I would like a baby brother." Annie finally said.

"Good." Laughed Martha. "But we don't yet know if

it will be a boy or girl. It will be a nice surprise, won't it."

Annie jumped around, asking questions about feeding and changing and looking after her new baby brother or sister.

When Fred returned each evening Martha would joke that she thought her ears would drop off, from the incessant chattering of the little girl. Fred would laugh delightedly, feeling the happiness that filled up the house.

A month before the baby was due, Fred decided to go back to the authorities to see what had happened about his complaint. They told him that several children had come forward when they'd heard that the workhouse was being investigated.

They had told of their beatings, one was only about eight years old when matron had beaten him three days in a row, for complaining about the bread being too hard to eat, another spoke of being kept in the darkness for a week or more, because he'd fallen asleep during evening meal.

Fred was horrified. Annie had spoken of being beaten, but he'd assumed it had been a few slaps, but apparently Mrs Price had had a birch broom which she used to remind the children of their manners.

While he was there, a young servant girl arrived to give evidence of her maltreatment. Fred was stood there as she gave over her name. His eyes lit up as he wondered if she might be the one.

"Did you have a friend called Annie there? He asked with a deep intake of breath.

The girl span around to him and narrowed her eyes.

"Why? What do you know of her?" She asked sharply.

As Fred explained, the girl's expression softened.

"I promised her that I'd visit her on my days off, but they went to their house in Gloucester and took me with them." She explained guiltily. "Is she okay?"

Fred nodded, not quite believing that he'd found Annie's friend and protector.

"We took her in off the streets." He told her. "Sarah, would you have time while you're in Bristol to meet up with Annie? I'm sure she'd like to tell you her story and hear what's been happening with you since you left the workhouse."

"I'd be delighted. In fact, I have the afternoon off. It was my first chance to come here and put forward my statement. What luck, meeting you here too."

"Could you come back with me now then? She won't be able to believe me if you don't." He said smiling.

Sarah nodded and he waited while she gave over her details. She then walked beside him back to his home, where Annie was helping Martha bake a cake for that evening. Fred stopped on the doorstep and turned to Sarah.

"You wait here, and I'll go in first. You come in after a minute or so, and surprise Annie." He said, as he pushed open the door.

Sarah was apprehensive. She'd only just met this man *and he could be anyone*, she thought, *but he seems respectable and he definitely knew I was a friend of Annie's. I'll take the chance. It's broad daylight after all,* she reminded herself as she took a deep breath and pushed the door open and stepped through.

"Surprise." Fred yelled as the door opened.

Annie and Martha looked around to see the young maid stood in their doorway.

"Annie, oh my, how you've grown." Exclaimed Sarah, not knowing whether to stay where she was or to go over the Annie.

Annie stood there with her mouth open for what

seemed an age, before running over and wrapping her arms around her dear friend in a tight embrace. As they swung around in delight, Martha scooted over to her husband, looking at him quizzically.

"Sarah?" She guessed. "Where did you find her?"

"She just turned up to give her statement while I was getting an update. What are the odds of that happening?"

Martha looked at him, with eyes out on stalks.

"A million to one?" She said, as a smiled started to spread across her face. "How lovely for Annie. Where's she been?"

"I'll let her explain everything. Why don't you put the kettle on. Maybe we'll have an early slice of that cake?" He said, patting on the behind as she went off to the stove.

The two girls chattered, and though Sarah was a few years older than Annie, Fred could see how close they were.

"Please forgive me." He heard Sarah say. "I couldn't come and see you. I know I said I would, but I was staying in Gloucestershire. It was impossible."

Annie had no idea where that was, but was not a

person to hold a grudge at the best of times. On seeing her dear friend, she forgot about any hardship she'd suffered after Sarah had disappeared.

"There's nothing to forgive." She replied quickly, shrugging off any bad memories that lingered.

Fred steered the two girls over to the table and as Martha poured them a cup of tea, Sarah told them all about the last twelve months. They'd only stayed in Bristol for a couple of days, before going up to their country home in Gloucestershire. She loved her new job and even had a young man who she was courting, who lived nearby.

"Now tell me all about you." She said to Annie. "How did you get here?" She said holding her arms out and looking around with a smile.

Annie told her about the bullying and her escape from the workhouse. Sarah's eyes closed as she remembered how bad it was. She felt a heaviness in her heart as she wished she'd been able to do something to help her dear friend.

"I'm so sorry." She said.

"For what, there was nothing you could do." Annie said bluntly.

"Anyway, it all ended up okay in the end. When I escaped and got to Wesleyfield, this kind woman told me about this factory. While I was trying to find a way in, I was caught by this nice man, who gave me a job." As she reached that stage of her story, her eyes became moist, and she struggled to continue.

"What is it?" Sarah asked, putting her hand on Annie's arm.

"I'm afraid her young friend there had an accident, he died." Fred said softly.

Sarah looked shocked.

"It was a dangerous job that Annie was doing." Fred continued.

"I'm glad you're not there now." Sarah said turning back to Annie.

"Me too." Said Annie wiping a tear from her eye.

"So how did you get from there to here?" Sarah asked, looking around at the three of them for answers.

"Did you catch her there?" She asked, looking at Fred.

"Kind of." Laughed Fred. "but it wasn't really like that."

"No, I ran away and he found me in the town square and asked me to come live with them." Annie said happily, as she realised how lucky she'd been.

"You deserve it." Said Sarah happily. "Who would have thought it would have worked out so well for both of us."

Annie smiled and picked up her spoon, nodding in agreement.

Fred and Martha left the two girls chatting until it was getting a little dusky outside.

"Hadn't you better be off?" Martha asked. "Not that we want rid of you, but I didn't know if you had to be back before nightfall." She added hastily.

Sarah smiled and stood up quickly.

"Thank you. Yes, I should be getting back. I said I would be back before it got dark. They'll worry about me. Will you write me, Annie?" She asked as she started across the room to the front door.

"Yes, of course. And you'll write me back?" Annie asked, still not believing that she'd found Sarah again.

"I will. Once a week." Sarah promised as she said her goodbyes and left.

"She seemed nice." Said Martha as she started

clearing away the cups.

"The best." Said Annie. "I'm so glad you found her." She said turning to Fred.

"Me too, Annie. Me too." He said as he sat back into his chair.

CHAPTER TWENTY THREE

Fred returned home that evening with a broadsheet. Martha looked at him in surprise. He didn't usually bother with a paper.

Occasionally, he might bring home one of those penny papers, with those awful stories in, but not a proper newspaper, she thought as she tried not to look too curious.

Eventually she couldn't contain herself any longer.

"Whats that you got there?" She asked.

Fred put the paper down and gave his wife his full attention.

"I saw the headlines as I passed by one of the news stands." He said. "They're about the workhouse, and the atrocities that happened there. The matron has been sacked and has been forbidden to ever work with children again. Isn't that good news?" He said smiling up at his wife.

Martha nodded in agreement.

"Here, I'll read you some of the less horrific bits" Fred said.

"An enquiry has taken place at Bristol this week, before the county magistrates, into several charges preferred against Miss Elizabeth Price, the matron of Stapleton Workhouse for cruelly beating several young pauper children of both sexes… I won't go on to say what she was accused of, suffice to say, it beggars belief, so it does."

"Do you think we should tell Annie?" Martha asked anxiously.

Fred furrowed his brow, as he was want to do when thinking something through.

"I think so." He said slowly. "Maybe it'll stop her nightmares?"

Martha smiled at her husband. "You might be right. But maybe we just tell her that she's been charged? I don't want her knowing what she's been accused of"

"I think she knows better than anyone." Fred reminded his wife. "But I agree. She doesn't need us mentioning them. We'll just tell her that the Matron won't be able to hurt anyone else."

Martha nodded and turned back to her stove and left Fred reading the rest of the newspaper article.

When Annie came in from playing with the children up the road, Fred patted to the chair next to him.

"Come sit down.' He said gently.

Annie looked at him thoughtfully. Father Fred was a man of few words and she could count on one hand the number of times he'd specifically asked her to sit with him.

She sat down gingerly and looked at the man next to her. *I can't believe how lucky I am for him to have found me and given me a home*, she thought as she watched him trying to organise his thoughts.

"Its about the workhouse." He said hesitantly.

Annie looked at him fearfully. She had a feeling that he was going to say something she didn't want to hear.

"Well, you know I went to the authorities?" He continued.

Annie nodded, unable to speak.

"Well, they looked into it and the lady who ran it…"

"Matron?" Annie interrupted.

"Yes, well…" Fred coughed. "Well, the thing is… well, she's been told to leave the workhouse and she's not allowed to ever work with children again. If she does and she gets found out, she'll go to jail."

Annie just stared at him for a few moments, as though she couldn't believe what she was hearing, but as the news sunk in, a wide smile spread across her face, her eyes lighting up with emotion.

"So she won't be hurting anyone any more?" She asked

"That's right." Said Fred. "It's good news isn't it?"

Annie nodded so hard, that Fred thought her head was going to fall off.

"Did you hear that Ma?" She said.

"I certainly did." Martha said, smiling at the little girl, who decided that she was Ma, but she wanted to call Fred, Father Fred. She remembered Annie telling them it was because she wasn't sure whether or not her birth Pa was still alive and she didn't feel right calling two people the same name.

"She's a funny little thing." Fred had said, after she'd

gone to bed.

"She's our funny little thing." Martha had replied with a giggle. She loved being called Ma, and couldn't wait for the baby to introduce itself to the world. Not long now, she thought, as she watched Annie with Fred.

As Annie went back to playing with her doll, Martha whispered to Fred, "Hopefully the nightmares will stop now."

Fred nodded as he looked at Annie happily sitting on the nearby rug.

CHAPTER TWENTY FOUR

"Everything will be all right, won't it Father Fred?" Annie asked as Fred paced nervously up and down the room.

Fred stopped and looked at her, doing his best to hide his anxiousness. Martha was in the next room with the midwife, waiting for the baby to make an appearance.

"Of course it will be. I'm just desperate to see them both." He said.

"Me too." Said Annie. "What do you think it will be?"

Fred looked at her confused. "What?"

"Boy or girl?" Annie asked patiently, secretly wondering if he knew anything about having babies.

babies.

Fred smiled. "I don't mind. As long as it's healthy." He told her.

"I'd like a brother, no a sister, no... Oh, I don't know." Said Annie breathlessly.

Fred laughed. At least the child was taking his mind off his concerns for a minute of two, though it wasn't too long, before he started pacing again, fretting as to how his wife was and hoping the ordeal would be over soon. *I don't think I can bear it,* he thought. *If it doesn't make an appearance soon Im going to barge in there and find out what's happening.*

Suddenly they heard a loud wail.

"What was that?" Annie said, scared.

"That was your new brother or sister." Said Fred, trying to suppress the nervous excitement that threatened to send him near crazy.

"Can we go in now?" Annie asked, desperate to see Ma and her new sibling.

Fred put his hand on her shoulder and gently squeezed.

"We just need to wait until we're invited in. They'll need to check out mother and baby first."

"What do they do?" Asked Annie curiously.

"I'm not sure. It's my first time too." Admitted Fred, raising his eyebrows and making Annie laugh.

A couple of minutes later, they heard footsteps on the stairs and the door opened.

"You can go up now." The midwife told them.

"You off now?" Fred asked.

"Yes, but I expect you want to see your wife and child. You can sort me out tomorrow, if you like?" She told him.

"And they're okay?" He asked apprehensively.

"They're both healthy." She said smiling as she pulled the door open and stepped outside.

Fred looked at Annie, as if afraid to go upstairs. They had waited so long for this day, that now it had come, he felt a little apprehensive.

"Can we go now?" She asked, hopping from one foot to the other, but waiting for him to take the lead.

Fred nodded and started towards the door. Annie slipped her small hand into his and smiled.

He led her up the stairs and onto the landing. He tapped nervously on the door.

"Yes?" Martha called out.

Fred walked in with Annie.

"Why did you knock?" Martha asked.

"I don't know." Fred said, feeling a little stupid.

Martha smiled at him. She knew exactly how he was feeling. She'd felt the same, just five minutes earlier when she'd been introduced to their new son.

"Come and say hello to your baby brother." She said to Annie.

Annie looked up at Fred, who nodded encouragingly at her. She let go of his hand and ran to the bedside. Looking down at the tiny bundle in Martha's arms, she gasped.

"He's so tiny." She said quietly.

"I know." Smiled Martha.

"And look at his little fingers."

"I know." Laughed Martha, delighted that Annie was showing such an interest in her new brother.

"What's his name?" She asked, looking first at Martha and then at Fred.

Martha looked at Fred, who nodded.

"We thought we'd call him Thomas."

"Like my friend?" Annie asked, the hairs on her arms standing on end.

"Just like your friend." Fred said smiling.

"Why doesn't he have any hair?" Annie asked, with a puzzled look on her face.

Fred laughed.

"Lots of babies aren't born with hair, but he'll soon have some. What do you think of him?"

"He's perfect." Annie said.

Fred and Martha nodded and looked at each other. *Yes, he was perfect,* they both thought in unison.

Other Books by this Author

The Scullery Maids Success

Fred has always had a cruel streak, but it only gets worse when he loses his job. Luckily for Jane her mother gets the worst of it. What will happen when Jane manages to find a way to escape?
Jane is a hardworking scullery maid whose life changes when she meets Billy who works at the nearby cotton mill and lives with his adopted parents.
Billy's never really thought about his real parents, but that all changes when his birth mother finds herself on the receiving end of a blackmailer.
The Morgan's of Osbourne House are wealthy and live a lifestyle that Jane and Billy could only dream of. Jane finds herself the target of the unwanted attentions of John Morgan, the only son.
Jane is devastated when her mother disappears, luckily for her there are people looking out for her. Will secrets tear Billy and Jane apart or can they overcome the past?

The Reluctant Departure

Emma and James eloped to escape from their father's plans for Emma to marry James' father. Now they are doing what they can to make ends meet, but can they survive the heartache that awaits them?
Emma has to adapt to the many changes that marrying James had meant for her. Rather than the high life that she's used to Emma now finds herself

having to take in ironing, just to put food on the table.
James feels protective of Emma. It was he who had persuaded her to run away with him, rather than marry his father. Now they have no money, and James is overwrought with guilt.
Tommy Holmes has provided a life line to Emma, and when things get to much Emma disappears, leaving James to assume the worst.
Will James' secret tear them apart or can they overcome the obstacles life has put in their way?

The Chaperone's Choice

When Eleanor's father dies, she has no choice but to take a position as a lady's companion to the young Lily Woodward.
Eleanor has to adapt to life as a chaperone, living in a large house, not quite a servant, but definitely not part of the family.
Floyd and Hugh are good friends and Floyd seems to be smitten with Eleanor, but is everything as it seems?
Lily is fighting for Floyd's attentions, but does he just see her as a younger sister?
When a long lost relative reveals themselves to Eleanor, she has to adapt to the big changes this discovery brings with it.
Will Eleanor have a chance to tell her true love how she feels, or is it too late?

The Motherless Child

When Anna's father dies, leaving her with a debt she must repay, she has no choice but to move in with her Uncle and his family
Growing up Anna always thought she would take over the family business but when the factory goes

up in smoke, Anna finds her life spiralling out of control

With her best friend forbidden to see her and her fiancé disappearing, Anna feels that she is all alone.

When she gets a new proposal of marriage she wonders if the offer is all that it seems, or is there an ulterior motive involved

With deceit and secrecy all around her, Anna doesn't know what to do for the best.

Having her uncle as her ally Anna finally starts to rebuild her life, but does she really have to go it alone?

Will Anna marry the man she loves, or will her sense of duty prevent her following her heart?

The Christmas Resolution

When her parents die in an explosion at the factory where they worked, Rosie has to take care of her younger sister.

Without enough money for the rent, Rosie decides that they will have more chance if they move to London to find work, but once they get there she wonders whether she might have made a mistake.

As Rosie's sister gets weaker, Rosie is desperate to find something for them to eat and is in danger of being arrested.

When a kind woman takes pity on her, she feels like her luck is changing, but not everyone feels that way.

Finding herself once more on the streets, Rosie doesn't know whether or not she'll survive this time.

Is she destined to a life of poverty or will the truth finally set her free.